Welcome to the February 2009 collection of Harlequin Presents!

This month read the final installment of Lynne Graham's trilogy VIRGIN BRIDES, ARROGANT HUSBANDS, *The Spanish Billionaire's Pregnant Wife.* Leandro Marquez ruthlessly stops at nothing to wed Molly when he discovers she's pregnant with his child! And don't miss the first part of our fabulous new series INTERNATIONAL BILLIONAIRES, which starts when shy, hardworking Holly is swept off her feet by the magnificent Prince Casper in Sarah Morgan's *The Prince's Waitress Wife.* Expect emotions to reach fever pitch in Carole Mortimer's *The Mediterranean Millionaire's Reluctant Mistress* when tycoon Alejandro is determined to claim his secret baby and possess Brynne in the process. And will an innocent plain Jane convince Sheikh Tair Al Sharif to let go of his mistrustful nature in Kim Lawrence's *Desert Prince, Defiant Virgin?* Business tycoon Santos Cordero is intent on seducing Alexa into a marriage of convenience in Kate Walker's *Cordero's Forced Bride,* while sexual tension heightens when Stefano seeks revenge after being left at the altar in Kate Hewitt's *The Italian's Bought Bride.* Be prepared for a battle of the sexes in Robyn Grady's *Confessions of a Millionaire's Mistress* as Celeste and Ben find they want the same thing in the bedroom…but different things from life! Plus, look out for Nicola Marsh's *The Boss's Bedroom Agenda,* in which a sizzling night spent together between Beth and her gorgeous new boss, Aidan, changes everything!

We'd love to hear what you think about Harlequin Presents. E-mail us at Presents@hmb.co.uk, or join in the discussions at www.iheartpresents.com and www.sensationalromance.blogspot.com, where you'll also find more information about books and authors!

kept for his
Pleasure

She's his mistress on demand!

Whether seduction takes place in his king-size bed, a five-star hotel, his office or beachside penthouse, these fabulously wealthy, charismatic and sexy men know how to keep a woman coming back for more! Commitment might not be high on his agenda—or even on it at all!

She's his mistress on demand—but when he wants her body *and* soul, he will be demanding a whole lot more! Dare we say it…even marriage!

Don't miss any books in this exciting miniseries from Harlequin Presents!

Robyn Grady

CONFESSIONS OF A MILLIONAIRE'S MISTRESS

kept for his
Pleasure

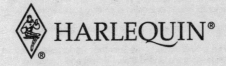

HARLEQUIN®

TORONTO • NEW YORK • LONDON
AMSTERDAM • PARIS • SYDNEY • HAMBURG
STOCKHOLM • ATHENS • TOKYO • MILAN • MADRID
PRAGUE • WARSAW • BUDAPEST • AUCKLAND

Recycling programs
for this product may
not exist in your area.

ISBN-13: 978-0-373-12801-3
ISBN-10:   0-373-12801-0

CONFESSIONS OF A MILLIONAIRE'S MISTRESS

First North American Publication 2009.

www.eHarlequin.com

Printed in U.S.A.

All about the author...
Robyn Grady

ROBYN GRADY received a book from her big
sister one Christmas long ago, and immediately
fell in love with *Cinderella.* Sprinklings of magic,
deepest wishes coming true—she was hooked!
Picture books with glass slippers later gave way
to romance novels and, more recently, the real-
life dream of writing for Harlequin Books.

After a fifteen-year career in television, Robyn
met her own modern-day hero. They live on
Australia's Sunshine Coast with their three little
princesses, two poodles and a cat called Tinkie.
She loves new shoes, worn jeans, lunches at
Moffat Beach and hanging out with her friends
on eHarlequin.

Learn about her latest releases at
www.robyngrady.com, and don't forget
to say hi. She'd love to hear from you!

To Mim and Jack for their wonderful inspiration.

With many thanks to my editor Kimberley Young,
for her encouragement and support, and
Bryony Green, for her fabulous suggestions.

CHAPTER ONE

'TRY to stay calm, but Mr Terrific-in-a-tux over there is undressing you with his eyes.'

Celeste Prince quietly grabbed her friend's arm and forced her to look away too.

'For heaven's sake, Brooke,' Celeste hissed under her breath, 'don't encourage him.'

Yes, the sexy stranger who'd just arrived was beyond intriguing. Neat dark hair, strong shadowed jaw, beautiful big shoulders that left her feeling a little weak at the knees. Superior specimens like that didn't magically appear every day. But, damn it, tonight she didn't need the distraction.

Over a hundred guests, all shimmering and crisp in their after-five wear, had gathered at the behest of Australia's franchise genius, Rodney Prince, to celebrate his company's twentieth successful year. But this soirée meant far more to Celeste than just another party. Tonight her father planned to step down as head of Prince Landscape Maintenance and hand over the Sydney empire's reins to his only child.

After her mother's death fifteen years ago, her dad had withdrawn from everything but business and they'd drifted apart. How she'd waited for this moment—the chance to be visible in his world again and make both her parents proud. Nothing mattered more.

Not even meeting that tall, dark, delectable dream.

Buckling, Celeste dared one more glance from beneath her lashes.

The stranger was leaning against a French door jamb, this side of the mansion's manicured court-yard. As his hand slid into his pocket his left leg bent and the ledge of those shoulders, magnificent in a white dinner jacket, slanted into a casual but confident pose. He was handsome in a rugged yet refined way, a toned powerhouse cloaked in classic Armani. However, his eyes mesmerised her the most...seductive pools of vibrant blue light. Captivating.

Aware.

Smiling straight into hers.

A bevy of exquisite tingles raced over her skin and she spun away again. Still she felt his heated gaze caressing her back, stroking her arms, slipping the satin straps from her shoulders, easing the dress all the way down...

Brooke tipped closer. 'Who do you think he is?'

Celeste tossed back a mouthful of chilled champagne. Her throat was suddenly parched. 'I don't know,' she replied, 'and I don't care.'

She needed to concentrate on reciting her acceptance speech without her cheeks turning into torches and her tongue tying itself in knots. "Stuttering Celeste" rarely made an appearance these days. After years of torment in junior school, she'd learned to slow down, think ahead and ease her way through most situations—even something as overwhelming as tonight.

Brooke arched a brow. 'You don't care, huh?' With one arm crossed beneath her gown's scarlet bodice, she rested her champagne flute near her cheek. 'We went through high school together, backpacked Europe together. Never once have I seen you this cagey over a man.'

Celeste couldn't smother a grin. 'Let's face it... he's not just *any* man.'

Drawn again, she glanced over a hitched shoulder. Like a cool-headed hit man, now the stranger was perusing the room, checking out the territory, assessing his targets. Such a composed air of indifference, yet she had the eeriest feeling he had his thumb on everyone's pulse...particularly the one beating a mouth-watering rhythm right between her—

'Celeste, I need to see you in private.'

Heart leaping, Celeste pivoted around to see her father's serious suntanned face gazing down at her.

When she'd arrived this afternoon he'd talked about the future of PLM, hinting again at his retirement and subtly sussing out her aspirations with regard to the company. Was she happy running the central Sydney handbag and accessory store she'd opened this year? Did she want to look at doing something more?

She'd replied that her profit margins were healthy. And, yes, she was definitely ready to do something new. No gushing or taking the words from his mouth, but clearly her father had wanted to confirm his decision before making the big announcement that had been coming for months. Soon the room would be toasting a new CEO.

Celeste Ann Prince.

Noticing that her stranger had disappeared into the crowd, she excused herself from Brooke and accompanied her father down a wide airy hall. As they passed the ethereal image of her mother's portrait, Celeste heard more clearly the crystals rustling around her evening gown's hem.

She'd considered wearing a smart black jacket and trousers ensemble, but had decided on the feminine look her mother had said suited her best. The peachy tone complemented her long Titian-blonde waves, and in no way challenged the last faint smattering of freckles that refused to leave her nose and shoulders. Anita Prince had said her daughter's sun kisses made her glow like an angel. She'd never understood that Celeste hadn't wanted to glow quite so much.

When they reached the study, her father shut the door on a room stacked with filing cabinets. He drew her towards his desk, then held her eyes with his. 'In ten minutes I'll make an announcement. I've given it a great deal of thought.'

Celeste gathered herself against rising excitement. 'I'm sure you have.'

'Prince Landscape Maintenance has grown into a huge enterprise…a swag of employees to oversee and organise. Master and subordinate franchises that need to be monitored. Its director should be involved at all levels, and can't be above driving a Bobcat or trimming a tree.'

Although Celeste nodded, her toes wriggled in their silver high heels. She didn't intend to be that hands-on; a great second-in-charge could handle any day-to-day grind. Rather she planned to invest her time in branching out to incorporate a chain of florists, which would accommodate only the biggest occasions, like celebrity weddings and gala events. She wanted the new section to be exclusive, cele-brated, in demand by the elite. It would be her personal contribution to the further development of the company. Under her leadership, they would reach even greater heights.

Her father crossed his arms. 'Papers need to be signed, but I've invited Mr Scott to stay a few days to help ease him in.'

Celeste's smile wilted. 'Who's Mr Scott?'

A new accountant? Lately, whenever she visited her father here at the office he ran from home, he'd been poring over the books, his face more lined than she could ever remember…and not merely from years spent in the sun. At sixty-five, he needed to relax and leave the toil to her.

'Mr Scott has enjoyed a meteoric financial rise these last five years,' her father went on. 'He's offered to buy Prince Landscape Maintenance. I thought you should meet him before I address our guests and share the news.'

The mahogany panelled walls warped and receded as her legs threatened to buckle and give way. She held her somersaulting stomach and forced the bitter-tasting words from her mouth.

'You want to sell our company to a *stranger*?'

She was hit by a frightening impulse to grab her father's tux lapels, shake him and shout, *Don't do this. You can't do this!* But she'd learned long ago that such displays of emotion got her nowhere. The last time she'd 'acted out', she'd been sent to boarding school. Thank heaven for Brooke.

Her father droned on about 'the generous offer' and 'everything working out well'. But Celeste could only think of how she'd always done what was expected of her. She'd excelled at school—even in reviled Maths—and had never attracted trouble while she'd waited in the wings.

How could he do this to her? More importantly, how could he do this to her mother?

She wouldn't hold her tongue. 'You knew I wanted to step in when you bowed out. We spoke about it just today.'

Her father's arms unravelled. 'Sweetheart, we talked about your handbag shop. I asked whether you'd thought about expanding.'

On the surface maybe. But the subtext had been there...hadn't it? Although she loved her shop, it was a placeholder business—somewhere to build on her university knowledge and practical skills until *this* happened. She constantly inquired about PLM, whether the franchises were growing, if there was anything at all she could do to help. Damn it, it had always been understood!

She grabbed at a likely buoy. 'You said no papers have been signed. Tell this Mr Scott you've changed your mind. That you're handing your daughter over the f-f-firm.'

While her cheeks caught fire, her father's brow lifted in surprise, then furrowed with mild disapproval at the stutter he hadn't heard in years.

He shook his head. 'This is best. It's a man's business, and, believe me, I've found the right man for the job.'

Celeste set her jaw. *She* was the only man…er, woman for the job. Besides robbing them of a chance to reconnect, selling PLM was tantamount to betraying her mother's memory. Anita had been yesterday's New-Age woman. She'd stayed so strong and had given so much, and she'd done it not only out of loyalty to her husband, but in the staunch belief that Celeste would benefit by taking over one day. Without her mother's sacrifices, frankly, the Prince franchise wouldn't exist.

A knock on the door echoed through the high-ceilinged room. Her father glanced over and raised his voice. 'Come in, Benton.'

Benton…? Benton Scott. Yes, the name rang a

bell. Exceedingly wealthy, rather an enigma. Big on charity but stayed well clear of the press.

Her free hand fisted by her side while the other clenched her flute's stem. She didn't care if Scott was a monk. PLM was hers. Watch out anyone who stood in her way.

But when the enemy entered, the oxygen seeped from her lungs until there was no air left to breathe.

That jacket. Those eyes. *Oh, Lord.*

Her tall dark delectable hit man.

His eyes met hers and widened at the same time he stopped dead.

So he'd been just as clueless about her identity when he'd given her the once-over earlier. Well, if he was still interested, so was she…in getting rid of him as fast as she could.

She jumped in to take advantage of the awkward moment. 'Sorry to sound rude, but my father and I are in the middle of an important discussion. Perhaps we could talk later.'

Her father went to protest, but perceptive Benton Scott held up a hand. 'It's fine, Rodney. This doesn't appear to be the best time for introductions. And possibly tonight isn't the night for announcements either.'

Celeste shivered. Those exquisite tingles again, but this time at a voice that was as rich and tempting as it was dangerous, like a stream of darkest chocolate undulating over jagged rock.

'No, no.' Rodney Prince moved toward his guest, his

five-ten stature minimised beside this other man's impressive height. 'Come through.' He flicked a glance at his daughter. 'We've finished here, haven't we, hon?'

Emotion thickened in her throat. Had he forgotten that much? Did her feelings matter so little?

Benton Scott spoke up. 'Actually, Rodney, I overheard a guest—Suzanne Simmons. She said she needed to find you to say goodbye. She'd already called for her car.'

Her father's moustache twitched and he cleared his throat. 'I should go. Ms Simmons is one of my most important clients.'

The younger man stepped aside. 'I understand.'

When her father clapped his guest on the back and left without a backward glance, Celeste braced herself against another twinge of hurt. But she didn't have time for self-pity. Savvy businesswomen didn't pout; they dealt the hand rather than merely played it. And, as much as it pained, Benton Scott could well be her trump card.

Outwardly cool, she concentrated on her words and indicated a leather tub chair. 'Please, take a seat.'

He smiled almost gently, then caught the door knob. 'As I said earlier, it's best we leave more thorough introductions for now. Goodnight, Miss Prince.'

No way. She had a plan and this man was her key. She needed to keep him here and talking.

She shot out the first ammunition that came to mind. 'Can't handle being alone with a woman?'

He stopped, then slowly turned. His grin was

lopsided and shamelessly sexy. 'That's never been my problem.'

Inventing an easy shrug, she moved towards the wet bar. 'There's always a first time.'

He leant against the door, one long leg bent, his fingers gripping the rim near his head. 'You look like a nice lady—'

'I noticed you doing some looking earlier.'

While her heart pogo-jumped in her chest—where had she found the nerve?—his hand fell from the jamb and he straightened. 'I didn't know you were Rodney's daughter.'

'That would've made a difference?'

A muscle in the sharp angle of his jaw began to tic. 'Perhaps.'

Her hand barely shook as she refilled her glass from an opened bottle set in a shiny silver bucket. She crunched the Bollinger back into its ice. 'Aside from being someone's daughter, I also have a double business degree. I run a successful concern of my own—Celestial Bags and Accessories,' she finished with a note of pride.

With what looked like a straight Scotch in his hand, he sauntered closer, a naturally languid and predatory gait. 'I'm suitably impressed.'

'Because I'm a woman?'

His eyes narrowed—amused or assessing? 'Because of your age.'

Good grief! She was tired of hearing about that too. Twenty-five was hardly a baby.

'I'm a determined person.' Gaining courage, she leant back against the polished oak bar. 'When I want something, I don't give in easily.'

He cocked a brow and Celeste relaxed a smidgeon more. Her bluff appeared to be working.

'And what is it that you want, Miss Prince?'

She took a breath. *Here goes.* 'I want to keep the family business in the family.'

After a considering moment, he squared his shoulders. 'We're being frank?'

'Of course.'

'Even if your father had thought to consider it, he wouldn't give you control.'

After the initial shock, she suppressed a growl. How dared he presume to know her family and their situation so well?

She placed her crystal flute on the bar ledge. 'It's not over till it's over, Mr Scott.'

His blue gaze turned steely. 'Your father's company is in financial straits.'

Her thoughts froze. That wasn't possible. They were one of the leading franchise businesses in the country. Had been for a long time. Her father hadn't had any financial problems since before her mother had died.

Benton Scott's voice penetrated the fog. 'Your father didn't want to worry you with it.'

I just bet he didn't.

She absently moved towards the open concertina doors as a wave of dread fell through her. But even if the company were in trouble, that wouldn't change her mind. A dip in profitability only meant that her innovative ideas were needed now more than ever.

But what did it mean to her hit man?

She rotated back. 'You're a successful investor. What do you want with a failing business?' Her stomach gripped as an answer dawned. 'Unless it's to sell off the assets.'

'I'm not a corporate raider. I see this company as a perfect opportunity to mix business with pleasure. Gambling on the stock market has been lucrative. But I want a business I can get involved with— pardon the pun—from the ground up.'

She studied him, from the top of his coal-black hair to the tips of his polished-Italian-leather shoes. Was she getting this right? 'You want to mow lawns and drive trucks?'

'As a matter of fact, when time permits, yes, I do. This company needs tender loving care for it to survive.'

She sent a dry look. 'And you're an expert on TLC?'

'In the right circumstances—' his gaze licked her lips '—absolutely.'

The tips of her breasts tightened as if he'd brushed each bead with the pad of his thumb. What could he do with a graze of his mouth, or the tickling tip of his tongue?

She swallowed against another hot rush of arousal.

Rewind, Celeste. Not in the plan, remember.

She crossed out onto the cool patio. Gazing at the fairy-tale spread of city lights and majestic arch of Sydney's Harbour Bridge twinkling in the distance, she considered her next move. When he joined her, the scent of earlier rain and damp eucalyptus leaves faded beneath the proximity of another influence… spicy, expensive and achingly male.

Out the corner of her eye, she saw Benton lift the Scotch to his lips. 'We're not going to agree,' he said.

'I disagree.'

He chuckled and turned to her. 'You're one stubborn woman.'

'I prefer the word persistent.'

She flicked a glance at his left hand. Of course no gold ring. Did he have a girlfriend? More likely he had several, which was fine with her.

Fine, fine, fine.

His eyes, reflecting light from the low slung moon, trailed her jaw. 'I wish we'd met under different circumstances. It could've been—'

'Mutually beneficial?'

He swirled his drink. 'That's one way to put it.'

'How about memorable? Meaningful?'

A corner of his mouth curved up as his brows nudged together. 'Why, Miss Prince, are you hitting on me?'

When his eyes twinkled again, her nipples tightened more and an alarmingly vivid image of his white teeth tugging one tip, then the other, bloomed in her mind.

Battling the sparks firing low in her belly, she cleared the huskiness from her throat and explained. 'Actually I'm suggesting you do the honourable thing and step away from this buyout.'

Disappointment dragged down his smile and he faced the view. 'Whatever you might believe, your father is being cruel to be kind. So am I. If this business takes one more wrong turn, you could lose everything.'

Sorry? Did she have 'walking business disaster' hanging from a sign on her back?

She crossed her arms. 'Thanks for the confidence boost. When I'm as successful as you are now, I only hope I'm as modest.'

His jaw tensed. 'Sarcasm is so predictable. I prefer it when you flirt.'

She huffed and mumbled, 'Well, you are a man.'

'And you're a woman,' he drawled. 'A beautiful woman, who obviously likes to wear pretty clothes and keep her nails buffed.' While her brain registered 'beautiful', the strong planes of his face softened. 'Why don't you take your share of the cash and buy a couple of boutiques to go with your handbag store?'

Her mouth dropped open. 'I'm not sure whether it's the sexist nature of your suggestion that rankles most, or the fact you sincerely mean that to be sage advice?'

Maybe he was bigger, wealthier…hell, maybe he *was* smarter than her. That didn't mean she couldn't fight for what was hers. Anita Prince would be cheering her daughter on all the way.

He considered her for a long moment. Then the mask cracked. He groaned and tugged an ear lobe. 'What are you proposing?'

She faced him full on. 'Compassion. You can buy any business you like but PLM is personal to me. My parents lost blood, sweat and tears getting it started.' She remembered the highs and lows as if it were yesterday—the flying champagne corks as well as the fights. 'You say you have our best interests at heart. Prove it. I know this business backward. Give me three months to show my father I can get the company back on its feet.'

The tugging on his mouth told her he was chewing his inside lip. After another nerve-racking delay, he exhaled. 'One month.'

Snap!

She hid a smile. 'Two.'

'Six weeks and with one condition. I'll be here, working beside you the whole time.'

'I don't need to have my hand held.'

'Plenty of damage can be done in six weeks. I have no intention of cleaning up any more mess than I need to.'

Her smile was tight. 'If I had thinner skin, I'd be insulted.'

She had to think fast. To have Benton Scott around would be far too distracting. For more reasons than one she needed her mind set on accomplishing her goal, not watching her back. Perhaps a different tack would dissuade him…something to make his super-sized ego jump.

She feigned a sigh. 'When I first saw you tonight, I assumed you were a man who enjoyed a challenge. A man who took risks. Guess I was wrong.'

When she turned away, he caught her wrist and flames leapt up her arm, colourful and consuming enough to ignite her body like a Roman candle. What was this guy's secret? Sex appeal pills with every meal?

Hoping the blistering effect didn't show on her face, she counted her heartbeats, then cautiously met his gaze.

While his eyes flashed, the grip on her arm eased. 'That's the deal. Take it or leave it. But something else needs to be out in the open.' He spoke to her lips. 'Six weeks is a long time. I'm not sure we can work that close for that long without…consequences.'

The innate heat radiating from his body toasted hypersensitive places Celeste hadn't realised she possessed—and had no intention of letting on she'd discovered.

She kept her words slow and even. 'You've come a long way since *this isn't the time for introductions.*'

'Don't get me wrong,' he continued as if she hadn't spoken. 'Consequences are fine. As long as you know I'm not after a *Mrs* Scott, no matter whose daughter I'm with. Or what that daughter wants.'

Celeste almost gasped. He was suggesting she'd

try to manipulate him into marriage to keep the business! How many times had Benton Scott had his face slapped this week? 'Sorry to disappoint you, but listen carefully...*I am not interested.*'

'No?'

She coughed out a laugh. *'No.'*

He chewed his inside lip again. 'I'm not convinced. Being a thorough as well as cynical man, before we go any further, I'll need to have proof.'

He left her no time to think. With a single arm he brought her near and like an apple falling to Earth—as if it was always meant to be—his mouth dropped and landed on hers.

The first few seconds were a blackout—all brain function shut down and energy funnelled to a suspended point a notch below zero. Then, as if waking from a coma, one by one every erogenous cell in her system zoomed up and blinked on. A heartbeat later, a ground-shaking surge of heat zapped like a lightning bolt right the way through her. When the palm high on her back pressed her closer, the intensity grew—brighter, hotter—until the magnetic inferno he'd created inside threatened to burn her alive.

This wasn't a kiss.

It was an assassination.

With skilled reluctance, he drew away, but only until the tip of his nose rested on hers. Caught in the prisms of his half mast eyes, she tried to make sense of her surroundings while her chest rose and fell, her limbs hung like lead and her core compressed around a tight, glowing coil of raw physical want.

When his head slanted as if he might kiss her again, she held her breath. But then his mouth hooked up at one side and he released her. Thank God she didn't teeter.

'I'm staying the week,' he said. 'If you're still interested—or was that *not* interested?—tomorrow we can talk more, perhaps over a drink.'

By some miracle she steadied her breathing and dredged up a smile.

'A drink sounds good. But just so we're clear, I'll take mine with plenty of ice.' She took his glass and pitched the warm Scotch over the rail. 'And so, Mr Scott, will you.'

CHAPTER TWO

EARLY the next morning, Ben Scott woke up face down on the sheets, hugging a comfortless pillow, painfully aware of a mean morning hard-on.

He cracked open one eye.

Strange room. No one beside him. Good Lord, he needed to roll over.

Taking the pillow with him, he groaned as spears of light spliced through the sheer blowing curtains. Then the night before flooded his mind, foremost his conversation with the irrepressible Miz Prince. Relaxing back, he closed his eyes and remembered their bombshell kiss and her clever parting remark.

He grinned. She wanted ice? More like she wanted gasoline poured on her fire. However, while he would very much like to help, common—and business—sense told him if he played too close to those flames, someone would likely get burned. He was here to take control of a high-profile business that needed an injection of funds and his undivided attention to bring it back from the edge. But if

Rodney Prince viewed this takeover as a saving grace, so did Ben. He couldn't wait to plunge in.

Soft laughter drifted in through his bedroom's second-storey doors. Setting the pillow aside, Ben strolled out onto the balcony. Celeste Prince was in the yard, ruffling the heads of two mid-sized poodles. When she threw a ball, they raced off like chocolate-brown rabbits across the wide-open lawn.

Crouched in the shade of an enormous Morton Bay fig tree, golden tresses framing her face, she might've been a fairy from the garden. Then she pushed up onto shapely long legs, her rounded cleavage popped into view, and those innocent thoughts flew from his mind.

He combed back his hair and, fingers thatched behind his head, stretched his arms and spine. While he'd been wrong to take advantage and kiss her last night, he couldn't regret it. In fact, if he had less moral fibre he'd do it again.

He finished his stretch, then cupped his hands around his mouth. 'Ahoy down there!'

She glanced up, but her widening gaze stopped short of reaching his eyes. Rather it got stuck on his bare chest, which suddenly felt twice its usual size. His mouth twitched. What was that about moral fibre?

Lowering his hands and setting them apart on the rail, he deliberately leaned forward. Realising what he'd done—given her a better look—she stiffened, then quickly dropped her gaze. When she peered back up, although her smile was controlled, her green eyes were glistening, just as they'd glistened last night.

'You're up early,' she said.

He thought of his crotch. 'I'm an early riser. Mind if I join you?'

'I was hoping you would.'

His brow lifted. 'I take it you're ready to get down to business.'

'I've never been more ready in my life.' She wound her arms up under that delectable bust. 'Let's do it.'

Thirty seconds later, Ben was face up under a cold shower, getting a good grip on himself.

He'd had women before. He'd respected and enjoyed every one. But, from the moment their eyes had met across the room, there'd been something different about Celeste Prince. He should've guessed she was Rodney's daughter. Later, in her father's study, he should've known she was laying a trap, leading him into a plan that would hopefully see him surrender his bid on the company.

He stepped from the shower recess and, dripping, grabbed a towel.

Yes, his normally clear sights had been blurred where Celeste was concerned. But he had her number now. She was a lady on a mission. He was in her way. She'd knock him down and drag him out any way she could.

He rubbed his chest and grinned.

It'd be fun letting her try.

Halfway out the front door, the thin middle-aged housekeeper caught up with him to hand over a note.

*Benton, an urgent personal matter has called
me away. Deepest apologies. Celeste is aware
and will make sure you're comfortable.
Rodney Prince.*

That bought Celeste a little time to think of a way
to explain this situation to her father, Ben thought,
pushing the note into his pocket and walking out
onto the veranda. It was clear she believed filling
Daddy's shoes would make him proud. Ben sympathised with her—even envied her a touch. He'd give
anything to have known a real father. A mother, too.

But he'd got something at least from his foster-
home days…a survival technique, which had later
crossed over into business: the uncanny ability to
quickly and accurately sum up people and situations.
Case in point, he had no doubt this deal would go
through; Rodney Prince would never entertain the
idea of passing on his ailing business to his pretty
young daughter.

And Celeste? She was all about deportment
classes and new season fashion. She didn't want to
accept it yet, but she was better off following her
more feminine sway. He was rarely wrong and he
sure wasn't wrong about that.

When he met Celeste in the yard, despite the cold
shower, the sight of her fresh face—those cute
freckles sprinkled over her nose—had his toes stiff-
ening in his heavy-duty boots.

He bent to ruffle both dogs' ears, then fixed the

Akubra hat on his head while she sauntered over, eyeing his khaki outfit. 'My, my, you're taking this seriously.'

'And while I like the frock,' he said, 'you don't look dressed for a day at work.'

Not a flinch. Only a measured reply. 'I thought we could go over the books. I can change into a suit if you prefer.'

Picturing her draped over a desk in a vest and tie and nothing else, he cleared his throat.

Focus, Scottie.

'*I* thought we should start by tackling the more practical side of things.' Eager to begin, he rubbed his hands together. 'Where's a mower?'

She smiled, a cheeky tilt of perfect plump lips. They'd tasted like cherries last night. The juiciest, ripest cherries he'd ever known.

'Are you going to give me a quiz?' she asked. 'You want me to name the parts?'

He copied her grin. 'Not quite. You said you could rescue this business. That you could prove you knew it all backwards. Why don't we start with something basic, like lopping an inch off this lawn?' He surveyed the grounds, patted his chest and inhaled. 'I can smell the petrol fumes and hot motor oil now.'

A dog came to sit either side of her as she stooped to slip an espadrille on each foot. 'If you're trying to deter me, save your breath. I was brought up on the aroma of fertiliser and grip of secateurs.'

He shrugged. 'Then you'll be able to show me a thing or two.'

'I didn't want to say it, but that's kind of my point.'

She strolled away, her derrière swaying a little too freely to be entirely unconscious. Ice, be damned. If her head was saying to concentrate on business, her body hadn't got the message yet.

She cast a look over one delicate shoulder. 'Are you sure you want to do this? You could always tell my father you needed more time to decide. I'll work around him and the situation, and when you check back in two months—'

'Six weeks.'

'Six weeks,' she conceded as he caught up, 'you'll see everything is going forward nicely and you can, in all good conscience, step away from the buy.'

'You mean do the *honourable* thing.'

She flashed him a toothpaste-ad smile. 'Precisely.'

He had his own ideas on how to approach Rodney with the subject of this 'trial'. But Celeste was right about one thing: she didn't give in easily. Pity for her, but he didn't give in at all. He wouldn't be fobbed off.

'Having me right alongside you was part of the deal, remember? Of course, if you'd like me to remind you again…'

Knowing full well what he alluded to—*the kiss*—she looked away, dropped her chin and quickened her pace.

He slipped his hands in his pockets. Interesting response. Was Celeste Prince a pussycat masquerading in vixen's clothing? Although that would make her easier to handle, he almost preferred it the other way. She'd been dead on when she'd said he liked a challenge—particularly one who kissed like she did.

She stopped before a large metal shed, then, putting her weight behind its sliding door, pushed until a row of lawnmowers was revealed. She waved a theatrical hand. 'Choose your poison.'

He let out a whistle. 'That's quite a selection.'

'Before my father started the franchise, he fixed mowers for a living. Now he collects them.'

'Like stamps, only bigger.'

She laughed. 'Something like that.'

Sauntering into the enclosure, which smelled of rags and dry lawn clippings, he fought the urge to kick a few tyres. 'This one should do the trick.'

Red and clearly well maintained, it reminded him of a model he'd used when he was a kid. He'd received a dollar whenever he'd tended the yard, but his foster dad's smile had been the best reward. He had only ever given praise, and had never raised his voice as some of the other 'dads' had. Six months into Ben's stay with his new family, that man had died of a heart attack. In his foster mother's red-rimmed eyes—in her overly kind voice—Ben had guessed his fate. Next house. Next family. Hell, by that time, he should've been used to it.

Celeste ran her hand over the metal handle. 'This one must be over twenty years old. Wouldn't you like a newer model?'

He wheeled it outside. 'This'll do fine.'

He stooped and ripped the cord. The engine whirred, but didn't kick over. Putting some back into it, he pulled again. Splutter, whir, then nothing. Seeing her dainty foot pegged out, but avoiding her eyes, he set his hat on the ground and yanked the cord almost out of its connection.

He smothered a wince and stood back. He would *not* rub his shoulder.

'It must be broken.'

Celeste sauntered forward and, with one perfectly manicured tip, flicked a small lever. Frowning, he looked closer.

The lever said 'Fuel'. How'd he miss that?

'Try it now,' she said.

He shifted his jaw, bent to rip the cord again and the motor roared to life.

With a solemn face, he nodded deeply. 'Good work,' he said over the noise.

Her eyes were laughing. 'Does that mean I pass the first test?'

He flexed a brow. 'I believe that was the *second* test.'

Her emerald eyes darkened but this time she didn't look away.

Pleased to have his vixen back, he settled his hands on the metal bar and remembered a vibration that shook all the way up to rattle his teeth. 'In your professional opinion, how long do you think this will take?'

'This model's not self-propelled, so the best part of the morning,' she called back.

He stepped away and indicated the mower. 'There you go.' Distaste dragging on her face, she stepped back too. 'What's wrong? You grew up with fertiliser and secateurs. You've mown a lawn before, surely.'

If he worked her hard enough, she'd be running off to her handbag shop by midweek. One day, she might even thank him.

She turned off the fuel. 'It's a large block. If you insist I do this, I'll use a ride-on.'

A few moments later, another engine was growling, a monster this time. A ride-on? This model was more like a tractor.

She found some gardening gloves and wriggled her French tips into each slot while he plonked his Akubra on her head. 'You'll need this. It's getting hot.'

Her chin tilted and she peered at him from beneath the overly large brim. 'Thanks.' Her tone said she wasn't sure she meant it.

After she'd pulled herself up behind the wheel, he hauled up behind her.

She rotated around, then ducked as his leg swung over her head. 'What the hell are you doing?

He squeezed down behind her on the adequate seat, tandem style. Nice fit. Nice perfume too. Light and flowery with a hint of a bite. Suited Miz Prince to a sassy tee.

'I told you last night. If we're doing this, I'll need to be your shadow.'

As if he had rabies, she shunted closer to the steering wheel. 'Perhaps you need a drink first. How's ice tea?'

'I prefer something hot in the morning.'

She turned fully around and sent him a warning glare from way beneath that Akubra brim. 'You won't scare me off.'

Well, hopefully not *too* soon.

He waved his hand at the steering wheel. 'Then I suggest you drive.'

Determination filled her eyes. She released the handbrake and planted her foot. The machine lurched forward and her hat flew in his face. Then she yanked the wheel, the tractor arced to the left and Ben fell sideways, barely managing to stay on.

Righting himself, he jammed the hat back on her head and, setting his hands on her hips, drove her rump back hard against his inner leg seams. She'd given him reason to hang on and her backside was the quintessential grip.

She slammed on the brake and scrambled off. When she threw the hat on the ground, he saw her face was flushed. 'I'm not doing this.'

He shrugged. 'You set the agenda.'

Talking him into this crazy plan, choosing this tractor, then trying to tip him off.

'You—you—' She bit her lip. Averting her gaze, she got her breath and maybe counted to three before she pinned him down again. 'You're not playing fair.'

'This isn't about what's fair. I'm doing what I need to do to ensure the welfare of a future investment.' *And, in due course, set you on your merry way.*

Her gaze zigzagged over his face as if trying to find a way in, or out. Then, with her mouth set, she pulled herself up on the ride-on again.

For the next hour they rode that baby in a diagonal pattern back and forth over the massive square of lawn. The vibration worked up his legs, rippling through every bone in his body. It should've been entirely non-sexual, but for her sweet behind planted before him…shifting, shaking, rubbing, until he gripped the seat either side and prayed for the torture to end. By the time they returned to the shed and she dismounted, his pants were on fire.

She grabbed the brim of his hat, flung it like a frisbee and set her hands on her hips. 'Satisfied?'

He groaned. *Not quite.*

He edged off the opposite side and held off rearranging himself. 'Well done,' he croaked.

'So, what's next on your agenda?'

'How about a long cold drink?' He turned to face her.

She looked half pleased. 'Possibly something with ice?'

He frowned. 'A man is not a camel, Miss Prince.' Nor was he a block of wood…well, not literally. At this precise moment, he was a desperately aroused animal who was a second away from showing her just *how* aroused he was.

Forcing his testosterone-driven brain to visualise a bleak snowy landscape—no valleys, no peaks—he headed towards the house, sensing the dogs padding behind him. When he slowed down, she caught up, but he steered the conversation towards a safe topic.

'How long have you had the dogs?'

'Matilda and Clancy were from the same litter. We got them…' Her words faded before she finished the sentence. 'Dad got them about fifteen years ago.'

He calculated. 'You would've been—'

'Ten,' she said, keeping her eyes dead ahead. 'Same year my mother passed away.'

His chest tightened, but his step didn't falter. Although, of course, he was 'sorry for her loss', in his opinion, that kind of phrase rarely sounded sincere. In her place, he wouldn't want to hear it. They didn't know each other well enough to ask about the circumstances. Instead he clicked his fingers and both dogs pranced up. Smiling, he brushed a palm over one wet nose, then the other. 'They act like pups.'

She swept her hair back in a temporary ponytail off her neck. 'They'll go and sleep under a tree half the day now.'

'They've had breakfast, then.'

Getting his hint, she smiled. 'I bet Denise has whipped up a feast. You look like a bacon-and-eggs man.'

His brows lifted. Good guess. 'And you say that because…'

She dropped the ponytail. 'I have a crystal ball.'

'A crystal ball would come in handy. Have you asked it about our six-week trial?'

As a warm breeze blew back the ribbons of her hair, he thought he saw her brow pinch. 'What do you think it would say?'

He didn't need a crystal ball to predict what would happen here. But suddenly he wasn't feeling so hot about playing a game that could only end one way. Even if he did step aside, Rodney would find another buyer. If, indeed, he *could* attract another decent bid for a business on the brink. Celeste was in a no win situation. Should he convince Rodney to allow her to continue with this doomed plan until she chose to walk away herself? Or would it be kinder to call stumps now? He knew from experience that holding onto fantasy could be worse than facing the truth. The sooner a person accepted, the sooner they could start to hold it together and survive another way.

When they entered the house, those thoughts evaporated as he soaked up the aroma of warm toast and, he was betting, fresh muffins. Man, he was starved. He was about to excuse himself and wash up when a familiar voice drifted down the hall.

Celeste turned to him with a curious gaze. 'My father's back.'

A female voice tinkled down to them next. 'Sounds like he's brought company.'

They found Rodney and his guest standing in the middle of the Axminster-carpeted living room, beneath the shifting reflections of a sparkling chandelier. From the night before, Ben recognised the woman. He wasn't the least surprised that Rodney was kissing her. He'd had the strongest feeling…

Celeste's hands flew to her mouth, but a gasp escaped.

Startled, Rodney broke the kiss and stepped back from the beautiful widow, Suzanne Simmons.

His moustache drooping, Rodney cleared his throat then rubbed the back of his neck. 'Celeste, Benton, you both know Mrs Simmons.'

Ben anticipated Celeste's reaction. He stepped closer, surreptitiously steadying her before her legs gave way. Ben nodded a greeting at the couple. Celeste couldn't manage the same courtesy. Who could blame her? This must be a shock.

Her voice was threadbare. 'What's going on?'

With her eyes on Ben and Celeste, Suzanne Simmons touched her beau's arm. Reassuring her, Rodney patted her hand, then walked up to his dazed daughter. 'Suzanne and I are going to be married, Celeste. We're very happy. Really looking forward to kicking back and having a family.'

Celeste's long lashes fluttered several times as she took it in. 'Dad, you're *sixty-five*.'

His jowls pinked up. 'Suzanne's having a baby. She's a fair way along with your little brother or sister. She had a scare last night but we've been to the doctor and everything appears to be fine.' He looked back at his bride-to-be and sent a smile. 'Just fine.'

While Ben felt Celeste's disbelief to his bones, he did what was expected. He put out his hand. 'Congratulations, Rodney.' He finished shaking and nodded towards Suzanne. 'I'm sure you'll be very happy.'

Another empty phrase, but this time, no doubt, appreciated. Ben believed in love wholeheartedly. It was the *happily ever afters* a man could never count on.

Suzanne's expression was kind and concerned as she came forward and took both Celeste's hands in hers. 'I'm sorry. This must be a huge surprise. We wanted to tell you tonight over a quiet family dinner.' The widow's gaze dropped to her rounded belly, then found Celeste's eyes again. 'I hope we can be friends.'

Ben's heart went out to Celeste as her slender throat bobbed up and down. Then she seemed to find some inner strength and somehow smiled. 'I'm... very happy...for you both.'

Suzanne addressed Ben. 'This buyout has come at the right time. We want to enjoy each other and the baby without the worry of a big business hanging over our heads.' She spoke to Celeste. 'Your dad tells me you'd like to buy another shop. That's so exciting. Bet you can't wait to get out there and start looking.'

Celeste's eyes glistened with a different kind of emotion as she looked to her father, who only looked away.

The circumstances were hardly the same and yet Ben felt Celeste's pain as if it were his own. It was a similar stab in the gut he'd experienced at age ten when he'd stepped one way, fate had stepped another, and suddenly he hadn't had that home any more. Guess the hurt of being pared off was no different no matter your age or position. Today at least he could do something to help.

Ben moved forward. 'I didn't expect to see you so soon, Rodney. I've invited your daughter out for the day. We were about to head off to grab something to eat.'

Rodney's expression jostled. 'Denise has a banquet on its way out.'

'And with my appetite—' Suzanne's settling hand found her fiancé's arm again '—I'm sure I could eat at least half of it. You two run along,' she encouraged Ben and Celeste. 'We'll see you both back here later.'

Five minutes on, Ben and the still stunned Celeste were seated in his SLK Mercedes, heading into town. She didn't protest; he'd bet she could barely talk. Her last twelve hours had been one kick in the gut after another. Yet she'd been so strong.

He was definitely no expert in fixing family woes; today he was an outsider, as always. He shouldn't feel responsible. This wasn't his doing. And yet what would it cost him to see his vixen smile again?

He planted his foot.

He knew just where to start.

CHAPTER THREE

BEHIND her sunglasses, Celeste gazed blindly out at the endless stretch of gum trees as Benton Scott's high-powered sports car propelled them away from her father's house. She didn't know if she ever wanted to see it again.

Benton didn't try to talk, for which she was grateful. Rather, with the top down, they drove until the traffic skirting the city slowed their escape. It was enough. She'd had an hour and had reached a conclusion.

Things happened for a reason. Today's king-hit was meant to make her see that the dream she'd held onto all these years hadn't been real—had never really been *hers*, no matter what she remembered from the past. Now it was time to either be eaten up by a sense of betrayal or let go. Given that her heart had been cracked wide open and all hope had leaked out, the second choice was a shoe-in. She had no more to give.

The well had run dry.

A traffic light blinked to red and Benton rolled the Merc to a stop. Exhaling fully, Celeste removed her glasses and studied the driver, who, at the moment, seemed more like a godsend than an assassin. Either way, he was the hottest man she'd ever met. And, it seemed, a sensitive one.

She half smiled. 'Thanks for getting me out of there.'

Glancing over, Benton pulled his mirror lenses down an inch, lifted a brow, then pushed the frames back up his aquiline nose. 'No problem.'

He was bad-boy handsome, perhaps with a touch of Mediterranean blood. His skin was smooth and olive, hair dark as pitch and long enough, she realised now, to lick the collar of his khaki shirt. She couldn't see his eyes so she focused on his profile…on his lips…beautiful lips for a man…dusty pink, the bottom one full and soft. She remembered how soft. Remembered how he'd tasted too.

'We're almost into the city.' He slipped into gear. The car cruised off again and the magnificent steel arch of Sydney Harbour Bridge came into view. 'I'd like to see your shop.'

Celeste smiled, but shook her head. Now he was taking compassion too far. 'You're not the least bit interested in handbags and belts.'

'Doesn't mean I'm not interested in what you normally do with your day.'

Brooke helped manage Celestial Bags and Accessories and had taken this weekend shift. They'd been best friends for ten years, but Celeste couldn't face her today. Knowing the family history, Brooke would try to comfort her and Celeste would sooner forget today had ever happened. A long hot bath and a good thick book might be the best place to start.

When the Merc rolled up to another set of lights, she turned to him. 'Sorry, but I'd rather you just drop me home.'

His large hands slid down opposing arcs of the sports steering wheel. 'No can do.'

She frowned. 'I beg your pardon?'

'The day's too nice to spend moping around inside.'

'I won't be moping.' Her frown deepened. 'I'm all done moping.'

He removed his glasses. His look said, Yeah, right. Aloud he said, 'I'll make you a deal.'

She gazed out the window. *Please, not now.* 'I'm not in the mood.'

'Not that I'm keeping score, but you owe me one. In fact, you owe me two.'

Her mouth pulled to one side. Oh, hell. She really did—for going along with her six-week scheme, and then pulling her out of that awkward situation with her father and Suzanne Simmons.

She held back a weary sigh and faced him. 'What is it?'

'I'll drop you home, but only to grab a swimsuit.'

Her pulse rate picked up. That sounded ominous. 'What do you have planned?'

He drew a zip across his lips. 'Federal secret.'

She had a flash of him entertaining her in a bubbling spa tub on the balcony of some glamorous penthouse suite. But somehow that didn't gel. She wasn't getting a 'take advantage of the poor girl while she's down' feeling. Rather the opposite.

Oh, what was she agonising over anyway? She'd bought a new swimsuit last week. She was a couple of kilos past her ideal weight, which had gone directly to her saddle bags. But what the heck? Would it kill her to be impulsive for a change?

Decided, she gave him directions to her apartment building, and ten minutes after he'd pulled up she was back down with her swimsuit packed. With his hip propped against the bonnet, he disconnected his cell call and opened her door, then eased back into his side.

He fired up the engine. 'Feeling any better?'

'I'm not feeling anything.' She shrugged. 'I feel kind of numb.' Must be a defence mechanism; it had been one of the worst days of her life.

He adjusted the rear-view mirror. 'Let's fix that.'

Soon the Merc was swerving into the private car park of a marina. A middle-aged woman with white-blonde hair and shortie-shorts rushed out from the boathouse to greet them and hand Benton a large picnic hamper. After thanking the woman, he escorted Celeste—a guiding hand on her elbow—down a jetty. They stopped before an impressive white yacht.

Her gaze ran over the lines of the hull and stopped

at the name written in red flowing letters—*Fortune*.
'I take it this is yours?'

When he removed the sunglasses, pride shone
from his eyes, which sparkled with flickering light
off the water. 'A beaut, isn't she?'

'Very nice, but I'd have imagined you with something bigger,' she teased.

He took her elbow again. 'Believe me, it's big
enough.'

On board, they changed—she into her tangerine
bikini and a sheer white beach shirt, Benton into
chinos and a surf vest-top that emphasised the musculature of those shoulders and glorious breadth of
his back. They stood side by side as he negotiated the
passage out and into the harbour.

Enjoying the fresh salty air pushing against her
face and the sun's warmth on her skin, she inhaled and
took in the stretch of glassy blue sea. What a difference a day made. Last night this man had been her
enemy.

Today?

Well, today she was a new woman with a range
of possibilities, including Benton Scott.

While he talked on about boating, she watched his
hair ripple with the breeze and admired the deep
brackets that formed around his mouth whenever he
laughed. Was Benton seeing anyone at the moment?
If so, it couldn't be a serious relationship. He'd said
he wasn't after marriage.

She pulled her hair from whipping around her face and studied him more closely as he spoke.

Was he avoiding a walk down the aisle because he was happy playing the field or for a different reason? Had anyone ever broken his heart? Somehow she didn't think so.

He steered into a tranquil cove and threw the anchor. The small stretch of deserted beach, which was enclosed by a curtain of rich green hillside, looked like a secret pocket in paradise.

After he dug out a picnic blanket and the hamper, he retrieved a bottle with an expensive label. 'Anyone for chilled champagne?'

She'd had enough bubbles last night. 'I'll stick to cola.'

He backed down the boarding stairs, then, extending a hand, helped her down too.

'Guess it's not a day for celebrating,' he said as they waded in knee-high water to the beach.

She thought it over.

'It is in a way. At least now I can start to move forward.'

They crossed to a shaded portion of sand and she helped him square out the rug.

'Do I get more than that abridged version?' he asked.

She flinched. 'It's a long, messy story.'

He rummaged in the hamper and handed over a cola. 'We've got all day.' He sat down, one arm resting on a raised knee, the other pegged out slightly behind him.

Celeste had kept the more sordid details of her past to herself, like a dog protecting a dirty bone. Brooke was her only confidante. But perhaps this was the ideal time to do a final purge and let it all out. But was it fitting to clear the air with the man who would soon own her parents' company?

Wrinkling her nose, she pressed the cool bottle against her chin. 'Are you sure you want to hear it all?' Was she sure she wanted to spill?

He examined the hamper's contents. 'We have sandwiches, cheese and fruit as well as chocolate hearts. Plenty of provisions to see us through till at least next Wednesday.'

She found a smile, but sobered again when she sat beside him and cast her mind back. *Here goes.*

'My father was a mechanic's son who'd become a mechanic himself, whereas my mother had come from money. You know that big house?'

He unscrewed a bottle of water. 'It's magnificent.'

'It was a wedding gift from my grandfather, who never thought Dad was good enough for his little girl. That put a lot of pressure on Dad, and when he began to gather more clients with his mower-repair service, my mother suggested he expand.'

She sat back, remembering snatches of those days like a favourite old movie. 'That time was the happiest I can remember. Dad was busy and productive and getting places, but he always had time for us.' She dug her cola bottle into the sand. 'Unfortunately his lack of business savvy got him into trouble with a partner who robbed him blind. He was devastated. That's when my mother got involved and pulled him out of the pit. She put together a business plan and asked for a loan from Grandpa, who wasn't at all pleased.' She drew up and hugged her knees. 'My father changed after that.'

Benton concentrated on her every word. 'Your father's pride was dented. When did you learn all this?'

'A child hears a lot when arguments are in full swing after bedtime. My father would want to do something with the business his way and my mother would warn against it. She usually won the toss. That is until the franchise was well established.' She hugged her legs tighter and peered out over the still water. 'I never heard my father acknowledge her efforts. In fact, I think some part of him resented it. Over time, the difference in background and lack of respect took its toll. All the love she'd had for him was gone by my tenth birthday.' She looked at Benton. 'You might not believe a child would know, but I could see it in her eyes.'

'No. I believe you.'

The deep understanding in his voice, the line between his brows, told her that he did, which gave her the heart to go on.

'The day of my birthday, I'd had friends over for a party and my mother, as always, held it together well. My grandfather had died the week before,' she explained. 'But when my mother sat down to kiss me goodnight, it all came out. She was riddled with shame and guilt and hurt. Grandpa had left all his money to her older brother. They'd never paid Grandpa back, it seemed. Dad had put it off and put it off. My mother was placated by only one thought—one day her pains would count for something when PLM passed onto me. Not that I cared about it back then. I only wanted my parents to love each other again.'

'But after your mother passed away, she didn't have any say in what your father did with the company.'

Or if he remarried and had more children. Celeste thought of the widow Simmons and the baby she carried. Guess she would have a brother or sister soon; she'd always wanted one. But right now she couldn't view those circumstances as simply as that.

She sighed and lowered her knees. 'My mother died of a cerebral haemorrhage. I was so lonely, I physically ached. The longer I was without her, the more important it became that her prediction that night would come true. More to the point, I couldn't see any reason why it wouldn't. But after this morning, that part of my life is over.' Her jaw clenched and she lifted her chin. 'I hate to admit it, but I'm relieved.'

When Benton dropped his gaze, her heart squeezed. 'Do you think she'd be disappointed in me giving up?'

Celeste wondered again about Benton's background. What skeletons he had in his closet. He looked so polished. So squeaky clean.

'Not at all,' he said. 'Your cause was a noble one. But I agree. You need to put that away and think about you now.'

She fell back onto the sand, hands behind her head, and stared at the vacant blue sky. 'I'm just not sure what it is I really need. Or even who I am any more.'

He lay down beside her, up on one elbow, his head propped in his hand. 'You're a young, beautiful, smart-mouthed woman who looks as fabulous in a swimsuit as she does an Akubra.'

Her cheeks heated and she grinned. 'Must admit, you looked pretty cute in khaki.'

'Didn't stop you from trying to pitch me off that ride-on. Good thing I have a firm grip.'

As they smiled her gaze wandered down the thick column of his throat, past the beating pulse in its hollow to the loose neckline of his top. His bare chest would be as hard as granite, but hot and human. Hot and wonderfully male.

A wave of intense arousal washed through her veins. Almost a reflex, she sat up quickly. The palm trees' shade had moved and the sun had crept up their legs. Heart pounding, she pushed to her feet. 'It's hot. I need to cool down.'

After shucking off her shirt, she waded into the water. But why had she run? Benton wasn't her enemy any more. The truth was she *wanted* him to touch her. Wanted it very much. She knew from the gleam in his eyes that he wanted that too.

When the water lapped her waist, she turned around. He'd taken off his chinos and, arms crossed, was pulling the shirt up over his head. Her breath caught. His bronzed athletic body, rippling with muscle, was a work of art in brief black swimmers. She'd seen that superb chest before, this morning on the balcony. But here, now, the extent of his masculinity almost overwhelmed her.

When he'd waded in to his thighs, he plunged under and, a few seconds later, surfaced inches away. He combed back his hair, leant forward and said, 'Boo.'

His biceps flexed as he dropped his arms and a thrill of anticipation gripped low in her tummy. His presence was so compelling it was nothing short of dangerous.

Should she play it safe—try to ignore their sizzling chemistry—or take a chance and lean forward too? She'd had a shock this morning. Was she in any frame of mind to accept and handle the consequences?

Still torn, she held her breath and dived away.

He was right behind her, holding her ankle and pulling her back so he could shoot ahead. Enjoying the endorphin rush and cool silk of the water on her skin, she dived on top of his back and pushed him under. When they came up for air, they were laughing. His hands were cupping her waist and, after the exercise, cords of golden brown sinew roped down the lengths of his arms.

Their smiles faded as the air between them

sparked with awareness—charged with sexual promise. Simmering with sensual need.

This time she didn't move away.

'Did you really think I'd try to seduce you to retain my father's firm?' she asked, finding her breath.

His hands slid down over her hips. 'I didn't know what to think, which is odd. I usually have no trouble reading people.'

She gingerly laid her palms on his pecs. Yes, indeed…hot human granite. 'Is reading people your special talent?'

His eyes darkened as his fingers combed down over her behind and his chest flexed beneath her hands. 'One of them.'

Her pulse rate picked up a notch. 'I'll admit it now. I liked your kiss.'

He grinned. 'I guessed.' He took her right hand and grazed his lips over the delicate underside of her wrist. 'You might be interested to know that my kissing abilities aren't limited to mouth to mouth.'

The buzz from that intimate contact was still humming through her blood when she found her voice, which had gone curiously thick. 'Give me an example.'

Feigning affront, he tipped his chin at her wrist. 'That's not proof enough?'

She gave a teasing shrug. 'Might've been a fluke.'

His thumb pressed into her palm, opening her fingers. 'Then let's try the mouth-to-fingertip technique.' He concentrated on each finger, placing his lips on their tips, sucking the last one into his mouth just a little.

Her core smouldered and sparked. Although she pretended indifference, she was breathing faster now. 'Hmm. Not bad.'

His sexy smile was knowing. 'Here's a personal favourite…lips trailing the curve of the neck.'

He came forward and her head rocked back as he nuzzled skin that was connected to invisible strings that made her nipples tingle and jump.

As he slowly pulled away she stifled a syrupy sigh but offered only a half-hearted nod. 'Quite nice, Mr Scott. But hardly inventive.'

His eyes narrowed playfully. 'You want new and exciting?'

'Are my expectations too high?'

'I don't know. Are they?'

She knew what he was asking. He wasn't into commitment. God knew, after today's kick in the pants, neither was she.

She coiled her arms around his neck. 'The last fifteen years of my life I've spent limiting myself. Never letting my eye roam from the target. Today hurt, but you're right. I need to put that behind me and do what's best for me now.' Her fingers threaded up through the strong wet hair at his nape. 'Are *you* what I need now?'

He brought her hips forward. 'I know you're what *I* need.' Beneath the water, she felt just how much.

Giving herself over to the delicious pulsing ache deep inside, she rested her lips against his. 'I think I'm ready to try mouth to mouth again.'

His eyes smiled. 'I'll see what I can do about new and exciting.'

CHAPTER FOUR

CELESTE let go any remaining inhibitions and met Benton's kiss, head-on. A jet of colour-filled emotions swirled through her, just as they had when his mouth had claimed hers to such devastating effect last night. But this time the thrill and desire felt sharper—went deeper. She trembled, thinking of what was to come.

Beneath the water line, those large masculine hands on her hips gently rotated her against his swell.

His arms wrapped around her more, then he brought her down with him until they were kissing underwater—all sound cut off, daylight flicking faraway patterns over their heads. When they ran out of air and surfaced, her bikini top was in his hand.

Gobsmacked, she gaped down. Yep, she was naked from the hips up.

With a testing grin, he dangled the top. 'Not sure how *that* happened. Hope you're not shy.'

Normally she was. She was a keep-the-lights-off

kind of girl. And she hadn't been with anyone for a good while. But no one had ever attracted her like this man. She could go on kissing him for ever. But since that wasn't possible, she'd gladly take every moment she had with him today.

So, after a small stab of embarrassment and a deep breath, she smiled. 'I'm feeling reckless.'

His blue eyes sparkled. 'Way better than feeling numb.'

He was about to kiss her again when she pulled back and threw a nervous glance over her shoulder. 'There's no one around, though, is there?'

His finger skimmed up her arm, then down to circle one tight nipple. '*Reckless*, remember.' He gently rolled the peak.

Melting at his touch, she couldn't find any words, particularly when he left her to stand alone as he sank beneath the water again. Feeling exposed, but resisting the urge to cover her bare breasts, she coughed out a laugh as she felt her bikini bottoms slipping down. A second later she quivered; she guessed it was his mouth that had brushed at the juncture of her thighs.

Benton emerged slowly…the top of his head, his eyes and nose, then his wicked smile. Standing before her like an eternal mountain, he dangled the bottoms. 'Still feeling brave.'

Yes. *No.*

Her stomach gripped. 'I've never done this before.'

His expression froze. 'You're a virgin?'

'I mean I've never slept with someone I've known less than a day.'

His hand combed over her crown, ending by tugging her hair, and head, gently back. He kissed her with a penetrating, calculated skill that curled her toes and left the tips of her breasts burning as they rubbed against his crisp chest hair.

His lips gradually left hers. 'Then I consider myself a very lucky man.' He took her hand and cupped it over his erection.

She felt her eyes bulge. 'Am I supposed to say I'm lucky, too?'

He growled. 'Right now, you're not supposed to say too much at all.'

He kissed her again, one hand on the small of her back pushing her against him as well as their hands sandwiched between. Then his hand turned and scooped between her thighs. His touch slid up her centre and down again, stoking the fire before honing in on that critical burning bead.

She groaned against his mouth. 'Can I just say that feels fabulous?'

'On one condition.' She felt the naked length of him jump and slide across her belly. 'I get to say the same.'

He bent so that his knees bracketed hers and lowered enough to guide his hot velvet tip over and around *that* spot.

His warm breath murmured at her ear, reducing her to compliant putty. 'Are you protected?'

She faded back up.

Protection? *Oh, damn!*

She bit her lip. 'Sorry.'

His knees straightened as he dropped soft lingering kisses on her cheek and brow. 'I have condoms on board.'

She quelled a pang of hurt. So he'd brought other women here, or at least had had women on his boat. How many? Two? Twenty?

Inside, she forced a shrug.

So they were both experienced—he a good deal more than she, no doubt—but what did she expect? More so, what did it matter when her body had caught light and real time had twirled off into another dimension?

He handed over her bikini, swung her up into the mighty bands of his arms and waded to the boarding steps. Then he gazed down at her, his mouth pressed together. 'Don't think I can manage the steps with you in my arms.'

Well, of course not. But she wasn't climbing up first. At least he still had his swimmers on.

'Put me down. I'll follow on behind.'

'I have a better idea.'

With a single fluid movement, he manoeuvred her body and flung her over the sturdy ledge of his shoulder, sack-of-potatoes style. Her naked butt was pointing in the air—*oh, God*—right next to his face. Clinging to the hard muscle of his sides—taking in the upside-down sight of his tight buns—she felt her cheeks burn unbearably hot.

'I'm not comfortable about this,' she cried out.

She felt his chest and back expand on a satisfied breath. 'I must confess I have an overwhelming urge to slap your tail.'

She threw one hand behind her. 'Don't you dare!'

His hearty chuckle reverberated all the way through her.

One arm pinned around her legs, he negotiated the stairs, then carried her to the front of the boat. But he detoured to a small bathroom and didn't set her down until he flicked on the tap. He kicked off his swimmers and, her heartbeat knocking against her ribs, her gaze slid down.

Oh, Lord!

But before she had time to think any longer on it, he ushered her into the shower recess, soaped up his hands and began to rub her all over. It was true. She'd died and gone to heaven.

She reached for the soap. 'Mind if I play?'

His touch slid lower. 'Join in any time.'

She pumped creamy liquid soap and while he lathered her tummy she palmed the gorgeous mounds of his shoulders. Her fingers wove down the middle of his chest, over his washboard abs, lower until…

She hesitated and he growled. 'Don't stop there.'

So she didn't.

The more she stroked and rubbed, the longer his eyes remained shut and the further his neck arced back. She was really getting the hang of it when, with a burst of energy, he seemed to come to. He smacked his hands on the glass either side of her head, the cords running down his neck strained.

His voice was a husky deep groan. 'I think you'd better stop now.'

They rinsed off, towelled off, then sped off to the bed, which wasn't king-sized but, in this case, size didn't matter.

He ripped back the covers and she crawled towards the middle. He pulled a blind on the oval window and the sky was shut out.

Way past eager, she flipped onto her back and he slid down over the length of her body until his lips grazed her left breast. He lovingly looped his tongue around the tip, then raked his teeth over the sensitive flesh until she was almost out of her skin.

Sizzling inside and out, she arched beneath him. 'I'll explode if you do that again.'

'What? You mean this?' He moved to her other breast and repeated the performance.

She pulled him up by his hair. 'Where. Are. The condoms?'

Soon he was sheathed and hovering above her again. When he eased in, her blood turned to fire and her bones liquefied to happy mush. As her nails skimmed his sides her hips bucked to meet his next thrust. The strength of him, the sheer power, felt so darn good...

'I think I might faint.'

Grinning, he pushed again. 'A few moments more.'

A few moments during which she discovered

where she belonged. In this incredible man's arms. In his bed. She wrapped her legs around his and clung onto sheer bliss. 'I know we're not finished, but can we do it again?'

She knew he would've laughed if he could spare the energy. From the hot look in his eyes as he gazed into hers, he was utilising every ounce of strength to hold back the tide. *Her* tide had already built to a shimmering, soul-lifting arc.

He pushed in deliciously deep, hit the right place with the right mind-tingling amount of pressure, and the rolling tidal wave crashed over her. Her centre contracted and the intensity erupted with the booming power of a bomb blast.

Flashing stars shot from her core, the pleasure-filled rhythm gripping and radiating out again and again. The sensations—the knowledge—felt almost *too* wonderful. She never wanted to let this feeling go.

Then it got better.

He drove in again. Every hardwired muscle in his body seemed to lock and tremble. The sound he made was almost one of pain that morphed into a throaty sigh as he plunged once more. Her fingers trailed up his arms as, eyes closed, she hummed out a dreamy smile that felt perfect on her face. Where had he been all her life?

She stilled at a flicker of regret.

Where would he be for the rest of it?

* * *

For the longest time afterwards, they lay in each other's arms, Benton holding her close against his hard body, her index finger weaving aimless patterns over his chest.

They seemed to fit…as if they'd once been physically joined and now both sides had been reunited. But that was her romantic imagination taking flight. Just as it was nonsense to believe she'd known his scent far longer than a day—clean and male. Real and intoxicating.

Later, when Benton suggested a swim, still feeling brave, Celeste followed his lead and skinny dipped in the cool revitalising ocean. They ate sandwiches and milk chocolate hearts on the beach, then made love again, this time leisurely, making the pleasure last, holding back the reward as long as possible…and the reward was twice as incredible second time round.

Benton's brand of bedroom skill was entirely inherent; the knowledge was as astute as the hands strumming the sweetest chords over her body. His pleasure in giving and receiving was sincere. Today she was the lucky one.

When the sun was a fiery ball sinking into the sea, they emerged from their boat bedroom cocoon. He'd whipped on his chinos. She was dressed in her white beach shirt and nothing else. She'd never been so casual with a man and yet today—with Benton—it felt only natural.

They each reclined back in a low slung canvas

deckchair, their arms hanging in between—fingers laced—and gazed up at the rapidly darkening sky, its horizon feathered with rose.

She laid her free hand behind her head. 'The stars are coming out.'

Had they always looked so beautiful? Tiny twinkling jewels that spoke to her. *Everything will be fine now,* they seemed to say.

'How do you feel?' he asked.

'Alive!'

His fingers squeezed hers. 'Good.'

'And also that this is a little uneven.'

He looked at her. 'Uneven how?'

'You know so much about me and I know nothing about you.'

She wanted to know *everything*, starting with when he'd learned to tie his shoes, right up to his plans for tomorrow. Had he ever had a long term relationship? Did he ever want to fall in love? But didn't everyone? That was what kept the human race going. Attraction, desire, a sense of belonging that culminated in two individuals becoming a couple. She'd seen the movies, read the books. But she'd never experienced the possibility of falling in love herself more clearly than this minute. He was indeed a hit man and she'd been slugged hard and fast.

'There's nothing much to know about me.'

As if. She turned more towards him. 'Try me.'

His laugh was short. 'There's not much of interest to tell.'

'You're being modest.'

He grinned. 'Why don't you use that crystal ball of yours?'

She searched his eyes before he looked back up at the sky and her stomach clenched. He wasn't being modest, not even mysterious. What was in his past that he was so reluctant to share? But if he didn't want to talk, it wasn't fair to push.

'I'm sorry,' she murmured. 'I didn't mean to pry.'

He found her gaze again, raked a hand through his hair, then scratched his head as if to stimulate the memories.

'Okay. Uninteresting fact number one. I grew up in foster care. Fact number two. When I was sixteen I got a job, finished my education at night school, then put myself through college. Fact three. At twenty-four I discovered the stock market. A year later I'd earned my first million. The rest, as they say, is history.'

A little dazed, Celeste tried to soak it all in. His childhood background was so not what she'd expected. She'd imagined a home something similar to her own, regular vacations, two parents who cared.

'Your mother?' she ventured.

'Died a few days after giving birth. No need to say you're sorry,' he said sincerely. 'It's not as if I knew her.'

And her heart went out to him for precisely that reason.

'What about your father?'

'Good question.'

'Your mother wasn't married?'

'She was. And divorced. Scott's my father's name.'

Celeste tried to keep up. 'You haven't tracked him down?' If she were him, she'd be eager to discover that connection—to know a link to her past. Maybe he got his looks from his father, his intelligence from his mother. Perhaps he had half-brothers or -sisters. What about grandparents? Didn't he want some answers?

'As a matter of fact, I've had a private investigator looking these past weeks. He's come up a blank. I thought about trying a different agency, but if my biological father didn't care back then, it's unlikely he'd care now.' He gazed at the sky and crossed his ankles. 'Sometimes people don't want to be found.'

His expression was meant to be light but his furrowed brow told her he was a little more than irritated. She understood, particularly if the PI's inability to track down his father was indeed a matter of the older Mr Scott not wishing to be found.

She studied his controlled face…the harder than usual line of his mouth.

Had Benton programmed himself not to care so the prospect of hope wouldn't eat him alive? Maybe that was why he'd been so sympathetic about her situation today. She'd held onto hope too. It hurt to let go, but she'd discovered that it would hurt more to cling on.

She searched for something supportive to say. 'I bet your father would be proud of you.'

His gaze still on the sky, he only offered a wry grin. Then his face broke into a genuine smile. 'Quick! Look there.'

She followed the line of his arm. A bullet shot across the blue-black sky, its silver tail trailing and fading behind.

Her hand went to her heart, which had leapt to her throat. 'A falling star! I've never seen one.'

She'd always wanted to.

'I've seen dozens. I used to watch out my bedroom windows, waiting.' He stopped as if he'd said too much, then he sat straighter. 'You're supposed to make a wish.'

Picturing a lonely little boy peering up at the stars, she squeezed her eyes closed and made a dual wish, for him and for her. As she opened her eyes he pushed out of his chair.

His eyes twinkled, reflecting the cabin's light. 'I know what you wished for.'

Perhaps half of it. But she wouldn't admit to anything. She didn't want him to know she was already close to addicted. To his smile. To his touch.

She lifted her chin. 'Let's hear it.'

He held up a finger—*just a minute*—and disappeared inside. Soon soft music filtered out. When he reappeared, a breathtaking masculine silhouette challenging the darkest blue sky, he helped her out of her chair.

Then he drew her towards him and began a slow dance, his chin resting lightly on her crown. 'You wished for a dance.'

She leant her cheek against his chest and bit her lip as emotion stung her nose. She'd never felt so special.

But was she? Was this 'just one night' or dared she hope for—*wish* for—more?

His deep voice rumbled through her. 'I'm glad we met.'

'Me, too.' Huge understatement.

'I promise I'll look after PLM.'

She closed her eyes at a sharp twinge but smothered it quickly. *Put it behind you.*

'I'm sure you will.'

He waltzed her around as the song's verse segued into the chorus.

'I'd like to keep in touch?'

Her heartbeat thumped so hard she was certain he could feel it jackhammering against her ribs. Difficult, but she kept her voice level. 'That would be nice.'

'Every quarter or so I can let you know how it's doing.'

Every three months? What was he talking about? Her pulse rate took a dive.

Of course, he was talking about her father's firm. Soon to be *his* firm. Not about keeping in touch with her on a personal level.

She set her jaw.

Get with the programme, Celeste. Benton Scott wasn't a man after a relationship. A little afternoon delight wouldn't change that. Certainly not a shooting star. And, after needing to give up PLM, she wasn't supposed to be in the mood for commitment either.

He rocked her around and pressed a kiss to the top of her head while the music played on. 'Would you like to stay the night?'

An honest answer? More than all the stardust in the universe!

But if she spent any more time in his arms—in his bed—it would be harder to leave, and it was already hard enough. This might have been casual, but the emotions he evoked were anything but blasé. Safer to go now and save her heart.

She filled her lungs. 'This was exactly what I needed. Thank you, Benton—'

'Call me Ben.'

She smiled. *Ben* suited him far better. 'I think I'll go home.'

Was it imagination, but she thought he held her a little tighter.

He grazed his chin near her temple and murmured, 'Let's finish this dance first.'

By the time the song ended, the words of the chorus were buried in her mind and heart for ever.

Yes. She had a feeling time would go by very slowly. But now it was time to move on.

CHAPTER FIVE

NEW YEAR'S EVE?

Bah Humbug.

Celeste sank into a chair at Sydney Airport's domestic terminal and set her chin in her hand. Moments ago, she'd said bon voyage to Brooke, who'd boarded a plane destined for romantic Hamilton Island on the Great Barrier Reef. Brooke had swung a great deal with a travel-agent friend; they'd both begged Celeste to come too. Luxury accommodation. Parties every night.

Celeste heaved a sigh.

She didn't have the energy. She would love to be waltzing around, totally fine with the world, but her rose-coloured glasses were smeared with grey. Though she wished she were stronger, she was still coming to terms with the ka-thunk of losing PLM. And then there was her other problem...

Sitting opposite, a middle aged man, wearing shorts, brown fuzzy socks and black sneakers, blew his bulbous nose into a chequered handkerchief.

Celeste cringed and shifted her gaze to a vending machine.

Her jetting off with Brooke and Pip would only bring their tone down. They deserved to have a good time, and if they happened to find someone nice who took them in his arms at midnight…

A skinny man with a concave chest and long hairy arms passed Celeste's line of vision and she flinched.

Well, good luck to *anyone* who got lucky tonight. But she didn't want to be put in that situation—a spritzer in one hand and some half-sozzled Neanderthal trying to get up close and personal on the other.

A rush of regret, wrapped in longing, spiralled through her tummy.

Celeste, you've screwed it for yourself.

Six weeks on from saying goodbye, every man she looked at left her feeling either ill or ambivalent. No one could even half measure up to Benton Scott.

Her nape tingled with a strange awareness, as if a warm breeze had brushed by her back. A second later she tingled at a murmur at her ear.

'Boo.'

Heart catapulting to her throat, she spun around in her seat. Every millilitre of blood dropped to her toes, then surged back up, leaving her slightly giddy. The lump in her throat was so big she could barely get the word out.

'Benton?'

As he rounded the row of seats to join her she battled the impulse to run over and throw her arms around his big beautiful neck. Instead she stood up, then almost had to sit back down again. He looked too good…

The pale blue jeans, which rode his lean hips, dressed those long muscular legs well enough to make her mouth water. His shirt sleeves were rolled halfway up powerful bronzed forearms, and the open collar revealed a tantalising vee of crisp dark hair. She imagined the plates of rock waiting beneath the white silk blend and memories of his scent filled her mind.

She'd thought she would never see him again! Yet here he was, stopping a mere foot away, his dazzling smile so broad and sexy, she worried her lips might not work if she tried to speak.

He pressed a kiss, which was way too brief, high on her cheek. 'I told you to call me Ben, remember?' he said, tipping back.

Oh, how she'd missed that dark-chocolate voice. 'Ben. Yes.' *I remember.*

'What are you doing here?' they said together.

Then, 'You first,' at the same time.

He laughed. 'After you.'

She gathered her thoughts and sucked down a settling breath. 'I've just seen Brooke off.'

'Brooke…your friend who helps manage the shop?'

She nodded. When he'd driven her home that night they'd talked about boarding school and Brooke, and how they were still best friends. He'd seemed interested but hadn't offered any more information about his past and she hadn't pushed, although her more curious side would've liked to.

'Brooke and another friend are on a week's vacation on Hamilton Island,' she explained.

He set his briefcase down. 'Should be one helluva party going off there tonight.' A frown pinched his brow. 'Why didn't you go?'

Slipping her hands behind her back, she crossed her fingers. 'I'll be busy with the shop—' she shrugged '—and things.'

'That's a shame. I imagine you could've done with the break.'

But if she'd boarded that plane, she'd have missed seeing him now. She'd daydreamed about just this sort of meeting, never believing it would ever come true.

She almost reached to stroke his hand, the hand that knew every responsive inch of her body. 'Where have you flown in from?'

Or, where was he flying out to?

What was the bet he was running late for his plane and had to rush off?

'I just got in from Perth.'

Excellent! But her smile dimmed. 'You must be exhausted.' Sydney was a six-hour flight from Perth, Australia's west coast capital city.

His gaze dipped to her lips before finding her eyes again. 'I've been in Perth since before Christmas.'

'Business?'

'Mixed with pleasure. A friend of mine wanted my opinion on some—' But he stopped. 'I must be holding you up. It's New Year's Eve. You'd have a party to go to.'

She'd had several offers but had declined every one. Same reason as Hamilton Island. She'd be about as much fun as a pregnant goldfish. But what excuse for being a sad sack could she pluck out of the air?

'I was going to have an early one, being so busy with work and all.'

His eyes narrowed. 'So you're tired?'

Backtrack, Celeste.

'Not *overly*.'

'It's just I've been invited to a party…' He waved a hand. 'Forget it.' He collected his briefcase. 'I'll get out of your hair.'

'You're not in my hair,' she piped up. 'I've got it up.' She flicked her ponytail. 'See?'

He laughed—that deep, rumbling, infectious sound—and she melted all over again. 'The party's in my building. Do you need to change?'

She assessed her black jersey dress and silver sequined flip-flops. 'I don't know. Do I?'

He caught her arm and a high-voltage sizzle shot over her skin. 'You look gorgeous.'

He only had to say it aloud and it was true. As they walked from the terminal she felt like the most beautiful woman alive. A woman whose day was suddenly painted in sunshine.

'So, you're Cindy?'

Celeste shook her head and called out her name again.

Reece, the man Ben had just introduced her to,

cupped his hand to his ear and shouted again over the head-pounding music. 'Was that Sheryl?'

Ben replied just as loudly. *'Celeste.'*

Reece raised his beer. 'Welcome, Celeste. Any friend of Ben's is a friend of mine. Help yourself to a drink.' He gyrated like Elvis. 'Have a dance.'

Celeste nodded but thought of the dance they'd shared on the deck of Ben's yacht. She was grateful for the invitation to the party…still, how she wished they were on that yacht now—alone, quiet, coming apart in each other's arms. Their unplanned meeting tonight was obviously meant to be.

But what did Fate have planned for tomorrow?

She thanked Reece and moved with Ben through the crowd to the small self-serve bar.

'Are all these people your friends?' she called out. They were packed like sardines.

He searched the room, then tipped forward. 'No.'

He withdrew a bottle from a sink full of ice, poured champagne, handed a glass to her, then raised his own. 'Here's to us.'

She smiled. 'To us.'

Whatever that meant. And she wouldn't find out here, with the music blaring louder than any night-club she'd visited and people crushing all around. But at least *he* was here and they were close and when the party was over—

A tall, lean man elbowed through and slapped Ben on the back. 'Benton, mate.'

Ben swung around and, with a shout of greeting,

shook the marginally shorter man's hand. 'Didn't know if we'd see you tonight.' Ben turned to Celeste. 'Malcolm, this is Celeste Prince.'

Malcolm affected a half bow. 'Pleased to make your acquaintance. I'll be even more pleased if you let me win some of my money back from your boyfriend. How about it, Ben? I'll let you break.'

While Celeste tried to get her mind around being thought of as Ben's girlfriend, her date shook his head. 'No pool tonight.'

Desperate, Malcolm clasped his hands beneath his goatee. 'One game. Just one.'

Ben was shaking his head when he saw Celeste nodding hers. 'I don't mind,' she called out. 'I like pool.'

Malcolm beamed and looped his arm through hers. 'Ben, your taste in women just keeps getting better.'

Malcolm meant it as a compliment, but Celeste remembered the supply of condoms on the boat. The circumstances surrounding that day six weeks ago had been unusual—feeling both freed from her past and somewhat lost about her future, she'd needed some TLC. She'd accepted his invitation, but had she been a fool to believe that the decision to make love had been her choice? Was it more realistic to admit that she'd been seduced by Ben's charm like, no doubt, many women before her?

Malcolm was already drawing Celeste away, calling over his shoulder to Ben, 'One hundred smackeroos down.'

Ben caught up. His gorgeous blue eyes quizzed hers. 'You sure? Watching eight ball isn't the kind of thing a woman wants to do in the hours leading up to New Year.'

She might have laughed. Ben could be a sweetheart, but he sure had his blinkers fixed when it came to stereotypical gender roles. Women weren't all about facials and pretty shoes and sexual conquest. At least she wasn't.

The noise halved when they entered and shut the door on a back room. A mid-sized pool table took up a large portion of the space.

Malcolm pulled a cue from the wall and chalked up. 'Balls are racked.' He waved a hand at the colourful triangle one end of the green felt. 'Your break, mate.'

Ben chose a cue and winked at Celeste. 'Malcolm and I have an understanding.'

Malcolm stroked his goatee. 'We play. He wins. But not this time.' He stabbed the air. 'This time you're toast.'

Celeste made herself comfortable on a stool and applauded when either man sank a ball. It was a good game but a quick game, with Ben the victor.

Malcolm propped his cue against the table and drove his hands through his thick red hair. 'One more,' he pleaded as he sped off around the table. Balls clicked as he hurriedly lifted them from their nets.

After popping his cue back in the wall rack, Ben rubbed his neck. 'Not tonight.'

Malcolm grabbed the triangle and set the balls up.

'Double or nothing. Celeste's a good sport. She won't mind.'

Having eased off the stool, Celeste appropriated Malcolm's cue. She lowered her back over the stick, closed one eye, took aim, and the balls smashed. Number ten flew into the right back pocket. She scuffed more chalk on the cue tip and blew. 'No, I won't mind. I like pool.'

Ben's wide gaze narrowed. Then he crossed his arms. 'Lucky break.'

She dropped another ball into the left back corner. 'If you say so.' She lined up and number nine slid into a middle pocket.

Ben coughed out a laugh. 'You can *play*?'

She visibly shuddered. 'Shocking, isn't it?'

Grinning, Malcolm backed up and dropped his hip over that stool. 'This is gonna be good.'

With a confident smirk, Ben racked the balls again. 'I'll let you break, Eddie Charlton.'

'I don't want to take an unfair advantage.'

Smiling, he squeezed her ribs as he passed. 'Just break, will you?'

She'd sunk six of her balls before Ben got a look in. At first he was confident, then he got anxious, now his mouth was a tight line of determination.

When she finally missed, he all but elbowed her out the way. 'My turn.'

Celeste rested her cheek against the upright stick. She was enjoying this way too much.

By the time Ben dropped all seven of his balls, a

sheen had broken out on his hairline. Lying over the cue, he closed one eye, sharpened his aim against the vee of his guiding hand, then, with a skilled gliding movement, connected the felt tip with the white ball. Celeste held her breath as white clicked on black, which rolled further away and closer to the far left pocket. A hair's breadth from plonking in, it stopped.

Ben straightened and blinked hard.

Far too tactful to punch the air—well, not just yet—Celeste put away her seventh ball, and took aim at the black while Ben knocked down the rest of his drink.

The sliding glass door, which led out to the balcony, whizzed open. A man, laughing and clearly inebriated, stumbled back into the room, thumped the table and the black rolled in.

Celeste swore, Ben smiled and Malcolm jumped off the stool.

'I'll rack up,' Malcolm said. 'My money's on Celeste.'

'We're done here, Malcolm,' Ben said, taking Celeste by the arm.

Ben guided Celeste out and the music hit them like a wall. He cringed, then leant near her ear. 'Do you want to stay?'

Not really, but she didn't want to go home either.

'What's the alternative?' she asked. He spoke, but over the music she couldn't hear. 'What?' He said something about fireworks. She shook her head and indicated her ear. 'Too loud.'

His mouth thinned into that determined line again

and he looped his arm through hers. They nodded goodbye to Reece as they headed out.

In the much quieter corridor, Ben thumbed the lift button and shucked back his shoulders. 'We can watch the fireworks from my balcony. Unless you'd rather go someplace else?'

His balcony? Meaning his apartment?

She wanted to *so* much. Her heartbeat was tripping out at the prospect of being entirely alone with him again, particularly after that competitive game of pool. Their adrenaline levels had spiked to a point where she felt as if they were ready to pounce on each other, which, on the surface, sounded divine.

But what about Ben's bad-boy charm? Had he thought about her these past six weeks even half as much as she'd thought about him, or had he pursued and enjoyed other women? The possibility of knowing Ben intimately again was as enthralling as it was dangerous, like leaping off a cliff blindfolded believing that she would be caught. But what if the reality was she didn't mean much more to him than a good lay?

Did she honestly want another one-night stand?

On the other hand, Ben had asked her to stay that night on his yacht; she'd been the one to decline and bid a convincing farewell. Maybe he would've phoned her otherwise.

Either way, couldn't she quit her over-thinking and simply enjoy this incredible man until she had to decide—if, in fact, it came to that?

She held herself tight and nodded. 'Your balcony sounds good.'

Two minutes later they entered a penthouse suite and she moved through into a living room that was tastefully decorated in light timber, black leather and arty stainless steel. She nodded. 'I'm impressed.'

While he hung his keys, she drifted towards floor-to-ceiling windows. In an hour, the bridge and harbour sky would fill with amazing explosions of colour. Each New Year the spectacle seemed to grow larger and last longer. This year was meant to be the biggest yet.

She sighed. 'The view from up here will be un-believable.'

The heat of his body closed in behind her, then he growled at her ear. 'Where did you learn to play eight ball like that?'

She grinned. That didn't take long.

She turned and tried not to sway when she found him so close, towering over her. His gaze was curious and amused. His mouth, lifted at one corner, looked way too tempting.

'My father taught me to play when I was young,' she said. 'I practised every afternoon for a year. There was a games room at the boarding school too.'

His eyebrows opened up. 'A *girls'* boarding school?'

She half laughed, half huffed. 'What is it with you?' She skirted around him. 'A woman's talents aren't limited to having babies and applying make-up, you know.'

He did know that…right?

'Are you saying you didn't expect me to be surprised when you sank those balls as easy as licking an ice cream?'

She almost buffed her nails. 'I hoped you would be.'

His eyes challenged hers as he sauntered over. 'What other surprises do you have in store?'

She couldn't think of any.

But she waved a hand. 'They wouldn't be surprises if I told you.'

'Tell me anyway.'

She cocked a brow. 'Can you handle it?'

'I can handle you.'

A spiral of delicious desire coiled around her core and squeezed. Talk about irresistible—as well as arrogant.

Smirking, she crossed her arms. 'Oh, you can, can you?'

His grin was so hot, it singed.

If she'd wondered before, she needn't now: he'd made his intentions clear. He wanted to pick up where they'd left off. And, in truth, she wanted him to wrap those strong arms around her, sweep her off her feet and kiss her until she didn't know what day it was. She'd thought often about being in Ben's bed again, but did she want to give him the satisfaction of handing herself over so easily? Which, it seemed, was precisely what he expected.

I can handle you.

He'd said it playfully, but he'd meant it just the same.

When he stepped towards her with that gleam in his eye, she ducked and moved out onto the balcony. By the time he joined her, she'd taken several calming breaths.

If she slept with Ben tonight, how much would it hurt if he didn't follow up their time together with a call? Of course, she could be honest and simply ask if he intended to see her again, but that presented a problem.

His response to 'are you going to call?' could leave her looking like a first-class fool. *You're great in bed, Celeste, but let's not get ahead of ourselves.* She would die!

He sidled up against her, his arm brushing hers, but she moved an inch away. She needed more time to sort out what she wanted out of tonight. Which meant veering her thoughts, as well as his, away from the possibility of sex. They needed another topic of conversation. Something safe, if not totally settled.

'I've been looking at starting plans for an exclusive florist service. It was something I wanted to combine with PLM, but…' She fought back the doubt and put on a brave face. 'I've had time to think, now I'm sure that's where I want to head.'

He gave her a congratulatory nudge. 'Hey, that's great. Have you told your dad?'

'I'm not ready. He offered to put up the money to buy another handbag store. But I didn't take it.'

Leaning one elbow on the railing, he studied her. 'Why not?'

It was difficult to explain without sounding ungrateful. 'For a start, expanding that way was his idea. And if my father gave me the money for the store, I'd feel as if it was his, not mine. Whatever I do, I want to go forward without anyone's influence weighting my decisions.' Whichever way she went, however she got there, the future would be hers—decisions, mistakes as well as rewards.

His voice was a comforting warm blanket. 'Your mother would be proud.'

She'd said the same to Ben, but about his father, when they'd spoken on his yacht that night. What must it be like never to have known either parent? Perhaps like missing out on knowing a piece of yourself. She couldn't imagine feeling that…*displaced*. And yet it hadn't stopped him from succeeding. Speaking of which…

Now was the time to bring it out in the open.

She put on a smile. 'How's the landscape maintenance going?'

The breeze picked up, bobbing a black curl on his forehead. 'It's going very well. The debt's all clear, I've spoken with all the franchisees, mowed a few lawns. Yeah, I'm happy.' His smile faded. 'How are you coping with it now?'

She pushed back her shoulders. 'I'm fine with it

being sold.' Liar. But hopefully one day soon. 'I'm glad Dad got a good deal.'

He searched her eyes. 'What about Rodney being a dad again?'

She sighed. 'That's still a little weird. I know I'll be happy when the baby comes. It'll be nice not to be an only child.' She shrugged. 'Better late than never.'

Pushing off the rail, he straightened to his full height and changed the subject. 'Do you want a drink?'

She changed it back. 'Have you ever wondered if you have brothers and sisters out there? Ever think of trying to contact them? Who knows? You might be an uncle by now.'

His smile was set. 'I'd rather not go there right now.' He clapped his hands on the rail. 'Want to help me throw together some salad? The housekeeper came in today to restock the fridge, and I've got a couple of steaks in the freezer I can defrost. I just realised, I'm starved.'

When he moved off, Celeste hung back. Ben knew nothing about his blood relations. Yet that hadn't stopped him from having a strong sense of self. On the other hand, she'd always clung to her familial totem pole. Now that pillar had, to a large degree, been taken away, she felt a little adrift. Tonight, her unsettled feelings for Ben hadn't helped. Could this go somewhere? If so, what did that mean for her future? A future that had seemed so clear-cut until six weeks ago, but now seemed up in the air.

She moved inside and made a place beside him

behind the tiger-striped granite bench. They stayed clear of talk about family while she sliced lettuce, tomato, shallots and Ben did his thing with rib fillet on a hot-plate grill.

He seemed to know his way around a kitchen pretty darn well.

'You cook for yourself often?'

'Most nights, sure. Pass the pepper.' He seasoned the meat, then flipped. Watching the steak—having the tasty aroma fill her lungs—she wondered if he did his own sauces. Something creamy. Maybe something spicy.

When her eyes lifted from the grill to Ben's mouth, her knife slipped.

'Ouch!' She jumped back and squeezed her finger.

Ben rushed over to inspect the wound. 'It's not deep.'

He guided her over to the sink and put her finger under gently running water. Still holding her hand, he retrieved a fresh towel from a bottom drawer. He patted the small cut, then found a first-aid kit and applied antiseptic with a cotton ball. A Band-Aid on top of that, then the best part.

His head lowered, his soft lips touched the spot and her breasts tingled to life. So small a gesture and yet it set her insides alight with an intensely pleasant heat. Was he aware of even half his effect on her? Smart answer was, of course.

He lowered her hand and slipped the steaks off the grill. 'They're overdone.'

'They'll be delicious.' Recovering, she tonged up the shallots and placed them in the bowl with the other salad. Then she wiggled her bandaged finger. 'Thanks for this.'

He flashed a teasing grin. 'Maybe I should cut your meat for you?'

'Do you want to feed me, too?'

It was a joke. Well, mostly. Still, she couldn't get out of her head the image of feeding each other, but not finishing their meal because the overwhelming sexual pull had them devouring each other instead.

He didn't answer but merely smiled that smile, collected their plates, and she followed him out onto the balcony with water and salad.

The meal was way better than anything she'd cooked lately. Leaving little on her plate, she fell back in her seat and dabbed her mouth with the linen napkin. 'You can cook for me any night.'

He refilled her water. 'Glad you enjoyed it.' Sipping from his own glass, he checked his watch and shifted back his chair. 'Almost midnight.'

She tried to swallow the nervy flutter in her throat with a mouthful of water. Of course he would kiss her—maybe lightly at first, but no doubt deepening until she was floating. But what would happen next? Would she give him the signal to advance? What if he didn't acknowledge it?

Oh, God, what if he did?

Escalating noise mushroomed all around. Whistles blowing, bells ringing, crowds hooting and singing.

Sydneyites loved New Year's Eve and this year their sparkling city had turned out in force. The tension on this balcony was just as combustible.

Her fingernails digging into her palms, she followed him to the railing. He checked his watch again, then studied the Harbour Bridge, which was set to ignite with transfixing kaleidoscopes of light at any moment.

Amidst the building excitement, he spoke, low and almost grave. 'In case you're wondering, I am going to kiss you.'

Her bones turned to jelly.

But she lifted a shoulder, let it drop. If he could tease so shamelessly, she could outright lie. 'I hadn't wondered at all.'

From way below, distant and near, the countdown drifted up.

Ten, nine, eight...

His fingers laced with hers as his face, dramatically cut in the moving light and shadow, came close. His next admission poured over her, hot and drugging. 'I've wanted to do this all night.'

Five, four, three...

How to react? What to say? She wanted his kiss, but how much, or little, did he want from her?

As she searched his eyes a roar of 'HAPPY NEW YEAR' went up and the sky erupted with loud bursts of colour-filled stars. While magical showers rained and thunderous cracks exploded all around, his hand, joined with hers, wound around her back and tugged her in.

He spoke close to her lips, his breath warm and inviting. 'Stars are shooting, Celeste. Make a wish.'

His physical presence was so strong—so close to hypnotic—she could barely catch her breath, let alone think. Her voice was tellingly husky. '*You* make a wish.'

His hand on the small of her back urged her closer. He was already hard. 'I wish you'd stay the night.'

Her skin was on fire. Her legs were loose rubber bands. What did she want? Where would this lead?

She groaned. 'I—I…I'm not sure.'

He smiled. 'Guess I'll have to convince you.' His lips tasted hers, tender and coaxing. '*Happy…*' another, longer taste '*…New…*'

Cupping her jaw, he kissed her slow and deep, with a scorching knowledge and soul-filled necessity that she'd dreamed of every night for weeks. When their mouths gently parted, he didn't say *Year*.

Instead, she sighed and said, '*Yes.*'

CHAPTER SIX

CELESTE didn't care if *yes* was the right decision. Lord knew it was the right decision for *now*. With fireworks whistling, bursting and collapsing all around, Ben smiled and led her from the balcony into his large shadowy bedroom. She followed, only knowing she was walking on moonbeams.

The smell of spent gunpowder drifted in through a giant open window. That, mingled with his masculine scent and indistinct shapes shifting over the walls, made the moment seem almost surreal. With flashes working over the strong planes and angles of his face, Ben kept his eyes on hers and effortlessly peeled the dress up over her head.

As he heeled off his shoes his gaze dipped and he smiled. She knew why.

Black underwear—a delicate crop top and scant panties. She could kiss Fate smack on the lips for guiding her hand in her drawer this afternoon when she'd dressed for her trek to the airport. She'd dreamed of standing before Ben Scott wearing her best French lace—but her fantasy hadn't gone this far…Ben corralling her back onto his bed, that devilish glint in his eyes, two minutes past the stroke of midnight.

As she reversed on all fours towards the middle of the mattress, he followed, unbuttoning his white collared shirt as he walked on his knees. When he reached her, he cupped her face and decimated her with a perfect-in-every-way, penetrating kiss. The stars falling outside had nothing on the wonderland going off in her mind and through her body. The only spectacle worth experiencing tonight was happening right here in this room.

When their mouths parted, he took warm, slow kisses from the line of her jaw. 'I've thought about you a lot, Celeste.'

Her insides jumped. One checkmark. Should she be so honest?

She combed her fingers over his shoulders. 'Me, too.'

She'd said those words before, on his yacht when they'd danced. He'd said he was glad that they'd met—*Me, too*—then he'd gone on to say he would take care of PLM. Soon after, they'd said goodbye. As days had grown into weeks it had seemed the farewell was final. Then tonight's miracle had landed in her lap.

His skilled mouth trailed down her neck and those memories floated off as a hot haze of desire built within her then condensed. She wouldn't think about anything other than the sensations she enjoyed this minute. Plenty of time later to dissect right from wrong. Not now. Not now…

She grabbed a corner of his shirt and coaxed the fabric from his shoulders. Her palms fanned over the human granite she adored, hotter and more vital than she'd remembered. In reply, he slid a thin, forgiving strap off her shoulder, then brought her close to adoringly taste the slope. 'I'm going to hold you to your promise.'

She fell into the heady splendour of his teeth grazing her neck. 'Hmm…what promise?'

'That you stay the night. *All* night.'

Fiery fingertips found the bottom edge of her top and, like the dress before, lifted it over her head. One arm bracing their weight, he eased her down, back onto the cool silky quilt. His touch was beyond exquisite. The way his fingers played her—over her hair, down her limbs—was a symphony fit for angels. When his mouth suctioned over one tight, pleading nipple, her lit fuse almost burst into a bonfire.

Her fingers knotted in his strong dark hair and she held him close. How on earth would she last?

'I like you best naked,' he murmured.

No one had ever spoken to her in that manner before—so sultry and commanding. And there wasn't a moment's doubt that she'd comply. Her breathing shallow, she lifted her legs and, quivering, closed her eyes. He caught a corner of her panties, and the black lace slipped up and over her pointed toes. She bit her lip against a whimper of pleasure as the edge of his hand sliced down…between her calves, lower to part her thighs, at last coming to rest at that pulsating hot divide.

She gripped the quilt as his expert touch wove in and around, driving the fire higher, compacting her passion to a finite beating force before—at the crucial moment—he broke contact and moved away. Breath rushing out, she snapped her eyes open and found his colossal silhouette kneeling before her.

Gripping her hips, he dragged until her legs draped over the thick steel of his thighs. Then he leant to scoop her up so they were positioned front to front with her sitting on his folded lap, her legs wrapped low around his hips, his length throbbing against her own burning need. His palms ironed up her sides before curling down her back, ultimately manoeuvring her behind until his shaft found an exquisite, heart-stopping way in. As his mouth claimed hers he began to move. She threaded her arms around his neck and trembled as the thrill and passion spiralled closer to out of control.

She'd been mad to think she might not want this. Tomorrow she'd survive whatever came. This minute she couldn't contemplate not having Ben Scott at least one more time.

Celeste drifted off to sleep around dawn and awoke to the rich aroma of freshly brewed coffee. Before she opened her eyes, she ran through her mental projector the sublime hours she'd spent in this bed. With *that* man.

Ben *Super Sexy* Scott.

She stretched and smiled.

Life certainly was wonderful.

'About time.'

At the cheerful greeting, her eyes sprang open. Wearing jeans and a white T-shirt, Ben strolled in holding a tray with coffee and something smelling of melted butter on the side.

She pulled herself up, feeling a little odd about bringing the sheet with her. He'd seen everything, *done* everything. There was nothing left to hide. And yet when he looked at her, all hot and expectant as he slid the breakfast tray onto a table, her cheeks burned. She felt freer with him than anyone she'd ever known. At the same time she'd never felt more vulnerable.

Last night was over. Tomorrow had begun. Where to now?

He held up a white ceramic coffee pot. 'Milk? Sugar? It's freshly brewed. Can't stand the instant stuff.'

Feeling like a princess, she told him how she liked it—hot and strong. When he joined her with two mugs and perched himself on the edge of the mattress, she had to fiddle to navigate a sip without her sheet falling.

He tasted from his mug then his index finger snaked out. 'What's this?' The tip of his finger curled around the top of the sheet and tugged.

Her respiratory rate jumped ten rungs, but she

didn't retrieve her cover. Rather, she held her breath, as she'd done that day in the ocean, and let the sheet fall in soft folds to her lap.

He looked deeply into her eyes. 'It's not about feeling reckless. It's about feeling comfortable knowing that you're beautiful. This morning, you're glowing.' He bent close, dotted a kiss on each breast, then found her lips and kissed her with more meaning than she'd ever known possible.

When he drew away, she wanted to drag him back. He affected her in a sense that defied words. It was as if she'd always known him and this was like coming home, sweet home. Was it the same for him?

Getting herself together, she nodded at the table. 'What's on the tray?'

He swallowed a long sip. 'English muffins. Your choice of honey, jam or Vegemite.'

She laughed. 'Now you're trying to spoil me.'

He twirled an imaginary moustache. 'All to serve my wicked purpose. We're going to eat in bed.'

'You're not afraid of crumbs?'

His grin was dry. 'I'll suffer it.'

He crossed the room and returned with the tray. When he was propped up beside her, long legs out, bare feet crossed, she plied more butter onto her muffin, poured honey till it was drowning, then sank her teeth in and savoured the sweet taste. She'd never enjoyed breakfast so much.

In between bites, they talked. Ben ate two halves to her one, then pushed the rest aside. 'I could eat more but I thought we might go for a walk and find somewhere nice for lunch, seeing it's after eleven.'

She choked on her food. 'Eleven o'clock!'

She'd been so preoccupied, chatting about the party and poor Malcolm and snatching glances at the musculature evident beneath Ben's T, she hadn't bothered to check her watch, or his.

'I've had a swim, pressed some weights, done some work.' His smile was curious. 'You looked too peaceful to wake.'

'I've usually done heaps by this time of day.'

'It was a pretty big night.'

She quivered to her toes. Big was right.

He trailed a finger around her cheek and kissed her with just the right amount of tenderness. 'Happy New Year, Celeste. I'd rip off my clothes and dive under there with you, but you probably need a break from my attentions.'

Uh, no. But that wasn't the right answer. She shouldn't sound overly eager after crumbling so easily and falling into bed with him last night.

Maybe a touch of the truth. 'I could use a shower.' She wanted to add, *After that I'm yours*.

But was she? This morning she was twice as keen on him as she'd been yesterday. She wanted to see him again. If she was unsure about some things in her life, she was certain about that. But if this was going nowhere—if last night had been a bit of fun on the side for Ben, nothing more—well, she would rather know now.

As if reading her thoughts, he quickly downed the rest of his coffee. 'There's fresh linen in the bathroom,' he said, nodding at the attached room. 'I'm afraid I can't offer you a fresh change of clothes.'

She brightened. Better than having a wardrobe full of dresses left behind by past lovers.

When he left, she dived from the bed under the shower. She felt revived and formidable when she emerged half an hour later. Ten minutes after that, she felt empowered strolling down an inner city street, her arm looped through his. Everyone seemed to smile as they passed. The grey had all gone away.

They found a Turkish café at The Rocks open for lunch and Celeste relaxed more over pide bread, zucchini puffs and home-made hummus. Ben was in great form and only stopped talking to listen with interest when she had something to say, which was often. When he told a story about dressing as Santa for his friend's children in Perth, and how his impromptu rendition of 'Jingle Bell Rock' on the front lawn had attracted every child and howling dog in the neighbourhood, she laughed so much her sides ached.

Afterwards they strolled again and window-shopped. It was getting late when Ben stopped and turned towards an interesting window. The bold black and gold letters said 'Magicians' Haven'. She was secretly admiring his sexy sandpaper jaw when he tipped his chin at a mysterious-looking orb on the lowest shelf.

'Is that yours?'

She looked down and laughed. 'My crystal ball?'

The ball's glass was clear yet somehow misty, flicked with colour that seemed to spark, then die away. The depths almost reminded her of her future—what once had seemed unclouded was now evolving, shifting, including what would happen next with Ben.

'It looks pretty authentic, doesn't it?' She half meant it.

He sucked in air between his teeth. 'Sorry. It doesn't convince me.'

'You think you could spot a fake from the real deal?'

'If there's any such thing.'

She had to ask. 'Do you think there *is* a real deal, Ben?'

He chuckled and squeezed her hand. 'I guess all those gypsies can't be wrong.'

This was it. He might yet ask to see her again, but nothing had been mentioned at lunch. Not, *How about a movie next week? Or, Are you doing anything next Friday night?* Wasn't that usually what happened when a 'date' was going well?

But times had changed. Women proposed to men. Females occupied top positions in business and politics. Wearing a skirt didn't equate to being considered a delicate flower any more. She wanted to know. If his answer was 'no' or 'let's see', she would deal with it.

'I didn't think we were talking about crystal balls any more,' she offered.

His brow knitted. 'What were we talking about?' But she could see in his eyes that he knew.

'Guess what I'm asking is…' *Say it. Say it.* 'Are we real, Ben?'

He didn't hesitate. 'What we shared last night was one-hundred-per-cent real.'

'And today?'

'If you're asking if I want to see you again, you bet I do. If you're asking if I want long term…' He paused, then shook his head. 'That won't change.'

She took his answer in and on one level was pleased. He wanted to see her again—that was comforting. But what did his statement say pared down? He liked being with her, sleeping with her, but if she was looking for more, he wasn't it—subject closed.

She brushed a wave from her brow and tried to smile, but her lips were trembling so much, she looked away instead. 'I see,' was all she got out.

They began to walk again and he blew out a breath. 'Look, you deserve an explanation—'

She held up a hand. *No need.* 'Point is we can see each other again, have a few laughs, play some pool…' Jump in the sack. 'Or not.'

She hadn't wanted to be left in the dark. It would've hurt far more to enjoy a few more dates, *then* learn they could never be anything more than 'casual'. Now more than ever she knew she liked Ben way too much to be little more than sleeping partners.

Her throat tightened.

How many others did he have?

Ben scratched his temple. 'The simple truth is, I'm not prepared to pick up a bow, take aim and see if I luck out and hit the bullseye with a happily ever after.'

She forced a laugh. 'Am I the bow or the bullseye?' She sure wasn't the happily ever after.

'I don't try to fool anyone into thinking I'm anything more than I am.' His jaw clenched and he seemed to think it through. 'Long term usually comes hand in hand with kids.'

Had she mentioned kids? Sure, like the rest of humankind, one day she planned on having one or two. But motherhood seemed a good while away yet. She had lots to accomplish.

'I wasn't planning on falling pregnant, Ben.'

His voice deepened. 'Of course not. No one should even consider bringing children into this world unless they're sure. And certain today isn't necessarily certain tomorrow.'

She shook her head. Talk about damaged.

She knew she shouldn't, but her concern and hurt slipped out anyway. 'You'll never get over growing up in foster care, will you?'

His smile was jaded. 'I don't mean to sound harsh, but you really had to be there.'

Celeste weathered the sting. She couldn't imagine having her earliest memories include dejection over feeling alone and largely unwanted. The father Ben had never known had abandoned him. But should he always let that regret dominate a big part of his life?

She might be disappointed in how their relationship had turned out, but she'd gone into it with her eyes wide open and, regardless, she still thought enough of Ben to hope that he'd find happiness eventually. However, it was pretty obvious that if he didn't move on, he would end up a lonely old man one day.

The cogs in her mind continued to turn as they walked on.

'Have you had any luck with that PI who was tracking down your father?' she asked artlessly.

Ben blinked twice at her, then lowered his chin. 'No. Nothing.'

She shrugged one shoulder. 'Maybe you should try that other agency you were talking about.'

He frowned as if she'd read his mind. 'I've been thinking about it. The first guy was a younger brother of a friend. Might be time for a professional.'

She hoped he'd be able to track down his father—his family—and try to make peace, if not with them, then with himself. She could easily hate her own father for so many reasons, but then she'd risk being filled with hatred herself; no one needed that. Both she and Ben needed to move on from yesterday and rob their pasts of the power to make choices for them—commitment issues included.

She stopped at the taxi rank. When she craned up on tiptoe to kiss his raspy cheek, tears swelled to prickle the backs of her eyes.

She forced herself to smile. 'Good luck.'

She moved to open the taxi door, but he caught her hand. His face was set. 'Don't go.'

Her heart cracked straight down the middle. 'Ben, I have to.'

A pulse jumped in his jaw as he searched her eyes.

'I'll call.'

She shook her head. 'Please don't.'

On the brink of falling in love with a man who couldn't commit wasn't where she needed to be. Poor Brooke had been in a similar situation last year. At least Ben had been up-front.

She slid into the back seat and gave the driver instructions. She wouldn't look back. Not once. Not a peek. But as the taxi turned the corner she jolted around and peered out the rear window. Ben was standing there, just the way she'd imagined.

Incredibly sexy and all alone.

CHAPTER SEVEN

BEN ignored everyone else standing in the room and moved up behind Celeste. Fighting the urge to wrap his arms around her slender waist, he leaned around her shoulder, brushing a kiss upon her soft warm cheek. She jumped, her back straightened, then she edged around.

As her gaze caught his, Ben's chest stirred at the telltale glow in her eyes…the familiar intoxicating scent of her skin. After a month apart, the magnetic pull was still there—stronger than before—heating his blood from the moment she'd walked into his packed boardroom thirty minutes earlier.

Despite the electricity arcing between them now, she slid one foot back and away from him. He understood her motivation. She thought it was over.

She was wrong.

Celeste swallowed and found her voice. 'Hello, Ben.'

He tipped his head. 'Glad you could make it.'

As their gazes lingered the current intensified and

the sexual pull cranked a notch higher, until Rodney, standing nearby, ended his conversation with a PLM franchisee from the southern district and rotated toward the couple.

Beaming, the former head of the company extended a hand. 'Benton, I appreciate today's invitation, though it wasn't necessary.'

Ben forced his attention away from Celeste's cherry-sweet mouth and shook Rodney's hand. 'I called today's meeting to bring all my franchise holders up to date, but I thought you'd enjoy being part of it and hearing about my initial push to expand.'

'Into Western Australia *and* New Zealand.' Rodney clapped Ben's arm. 'Well done, son.'

Ben sensed more than saw Celeste flinch.

So she still carried a flame for PLM. Last time they'd spoken, she'd had plans aside from her handbag shop—a florist venture. He'd hoped that would help her deal with PLM's change of hands, although, to be fair, it couldn't be easy.

Striking an interested pose, Rodney crossed his arms over his suit jacket. 'So, what's next for PLM?'

'It's early days yet,' Ben replied. 'But I have other development strategies I hope to incorporate while having some fun with this first expansion.'

Another flinch from Celeste.

Ben slipped a hand into a trouser pocket. They needed to talk. Alone. He had plenty to communicate and none of it involved business.

Rodney called out a greeting and waved to someone across the broad expanse of the room. 'Will you excuse me? James Miller looks like he's about to leave. He was my first franchisee to come on board. Lots of history there.'

Ben happily stepped aside. 'Be my guest.'

As Rodney moved off Ben wasted no time claiming Celeste's elbow.

Taken aback, she examined his hold on her arm as he walked her towards a set of double oak doors.

'Did I agree to go somewhere?'

He opened the door and ushered her inside his adjoining penthouse office. 'We need some privacy.'

'You didn't call this meeting to speak with me.'

Not entirely. 'I've spoken to everyone I need to.'

Now it was time for *them*. He'd delayed this reunion long enough.

He shut the door and turned the lock while she tugged down the hem of her classic black jacket. The matching skirt was a little long. The blouse buttoned too high. In fact, he'd just as soon pry every article of clothing from her body—lingerie included—but they needed to talk before they could move on to rekindling more intimate contact.

He crossed to his desk. Thumbing on the intercom, he spoke to his secretary. 'Lin, if anyone asks, I have an urgent matter to attend to.'

Celeste raised her brows. 'I'm the urgent matter.'

Sauntering back, he nodded.

As she perhaps understood more clearly his

intent, her eyes widened. 'My father…he'll wonder where I've got to.'

'Your father is in his element. He won't miss you for the moment.' Halfway to his target, he removed his jacket, tossing it on the leather settee as he passed.

Her eyes rounded more, but she held her ground. 'In case you have the wrong idea, I didn't intend to accept your invitation. I'm here only because Suzanne wasn't feeling well and asked if I'd keep my father company.'

He stopped inches away, deliberately looking down as she peered up. She was petite, yet luscious and entirely feminine. The perfect fit for his arms.

'You weren't the least bit curious to see me again.'

She looked away. 'That's irrelevant.'

Not in his book.

Two fingers trailed her cheek, crooking under her chin and lifting it high. His gaze drank in her lips. 'I haven't stopped thinking about you since you left me standing on that street corner.'

Had she done it to torment him? To tame him? Either way, today he intended to break the deadlock wide open.

His voice lowered to a growl. 'I missed you.'

She visibly shivered and bit her lip the way she had New Year's Eve when his tongue had trailed down between her breasts, around her navel and lower until she'd clung to his head and begged him not to stop.

'Ben, please…don't play games.'

He smiled. 'You like our games.'

On a groan she wound away and towards the door. 'I need to go.'

'Don't you want to hear my news?'

Her hand found the lock and twisted. 'I've heard enough.'

'I found my father.'

She froze. After a moment, she faced him.

'He's a retired teacher,' he explained, 'married with seven kids. I knocked on his front door, he opened it in a faded football jersey. A boy, about five, was standing behind him.'

'A grandson?'

'They were about to go out and kick a ball. He didn't know about me. His dentures almost fell out his mouth when I told him who I was.'

She drifted nearer. 'Didn't know about you? I don't understand.'

He strolled forward, closing the gap. 'Apparently he hadn't known my mother was pregnant. He wasn't in the country when I was born. They must have tried to track him down but gave up. Guess it didn't help that he took on his new wife's surname and became Bartley-Scott.' Although, knowing the system, he wouldn't hand out any gold stars that they'd tried too hard.

The crease between her brows eased. 'And you like him? He likes you?'

'Pretty much instantly.' He scratched his temple. 'Although his wife and their eldest let me know they weren't sure about a stranger turning up on their doorstep claiming to be a long-lost son and brother.'

She winced. 'That must've been hard.'

Years ago, whenever he'd been dumped at a new 'home' or had started at yet another school with shoes two sizes too big, he'd only ever imagined a reunion with his 'family' involving open arms. He should've known reality wouldn't be all rainbows and sunshine.

'The second eldest is tying the knot this weekend,' he went on. 'Christopher is marrying Marie, a lovely girl who, five-year-old Zack tells me, can whistle through her nose.' Celeste laughed. 'Despite two disapproving glares directed my way across the dining-room table, Gerard, my father, and Chris invited me along. The invitation's for two.'

The penny dropped and her jaw unhinged. 'You want me to go? Isn't there someone else you'd rather take?'

His frown was teasing. 'Don't tell me you don't like weddings.'

'You know that's not it.'

'It'll be an excuse to buy a new dress.'

She hesitated, then shook her head.

His arm snaked around her hip. She stiffened, but didn't move away. Good, because he wasn't in a mood to take no for an answer.

He moved closer. 'Celeste, I want to dance with you again.' *Be with you again.* This tug was maddening. Hadn't she been in hell too? His mouth dropped lower. 'Say yes.'

Despite her stand four weeks ago, this charge zapping between them proved it: they didn't need to go their separate ways. They were both adults. Why not continue to enjoy each other for as long as it lasted? There was no harm in that—only advantages.

Her face pinched. 'Ben, I can't.'

He searched her eyes. Time to reveal his ace. 'I've told my family about you. They want to meet you.'

Celeste held her breath. Had she heard correctly? 'You told them about *me*?'

His sexy heavy-lidded gaze roamed her face, raking the coals already burning deep and low inside. 'I sure did.'

Her throat bobbed on an involuntary swallow. 'You want me to meet your *family*?'

He cocked a speculative brow. 'Is that a yes?'

Celeste pressed her lips together.

Had a night passed when she hadn't dreamed about this man? Or woken remembering how alive she'd felt whenever she'd been with him? In his car, in his boat, in his bed. But she'd stayed strong, refusing to call him, blocking from her mind the reckless hope that *he* might call *her*. Then last week, she—along with her father and Suzanne—had received an invite to today's meeting. She'd been determined not to come. She needed to forget about PLM—about Ben—and get on with her life.

But how could she when she'd been a week late and had begun to worry? Yesterday made two weeks.

This morning, she'd bought a home pregnancy kit. 'Celeste?'

At his questioning gaze, a spear of anxiety sailed through her centre. She'd chickened out performing the test. But if she were pregnant she couldn't ignore it—or keep it a secret—not that she'd want to. She'd have to tell him. Given Ben's concrete view on bringing children into the world—that both parties should be ir-revocably committed—he wouldn't be pleased.

She chewed her lip.

But he *had* asked her to this wedding—and not just any wedding, but his newly found brother's. Despite her ambivalence about seeing him again, she wanted that experience to be memorable for him. Feeling connected was what Ben needed most, even if he wasn't fully aware of it yet. If he'd made this contact with his father, if he wanted her to be part of a family celebration, wasn't that a good sign? Wasn't there a chance…a chance they could talk, if nothing else?

Finally she let go a breath and nodded. 'What time should I expect you?'

A slow smile lit his eyes. 'Wedding's on Saturday at three. I'll collect you at two.'

It was done.

'I'll be ready.' She moved to leave. 'Now I really should be going—'

'There's one more thing.'

A strong arm coiled around her waist and tugged her back. Caught unawares with her defences down, she accepted his kiss like long-parched earth welcomed life-giving rain. She soaked up the texture and taste of him and with every passing moment only wanted more.

When their lips parted, she felt giddy. Worse, she knew her heart would be there in her eyes.

Damn the man.

Although her voice was thick, she managed to sound vaguely disapproving. 'I didn't say you could kiss me.'

'You must know by now—' he flicked the button at her waist and eased the jacket off her shoulders '—I don't ask.'

Her heart jumped to her throat. What was he doing? '*Ben*, you have a room full of people out there.'

His smouldering gaze hesitated, then lifted from the curve of her throat to her eyes. With a guttural sound, he replaced his hungry look with a frown and straightened. He slipped the jacket back up onto her shoulders and, jaw tight, led her to the door. 'Go join your father. I'll grab my jacket and be out in a minute.'

She smothered the sting of disappointment. It was goodbye again—for now.

'Then I'll see you later in the week.' When his frown deepened, she explained. 'I have to leave now to inspect my new shop fittings.'

His brows lifted. 'Sounds like fun.'

Well, she thought so. 'I need to give the okay on the cabinets and electrical—' She stopped. He'd gone to collect and shuck back into his jacket.

'Is it nearby, or will we drive?' he asked.

She coughed out a laugh. 'You can't come. You have work to do.' People to entertain.

Joining her, he lifted his chin and straightened the knot in his tie. 'I'm the boss. I get to punch my own clock.' He opened the door and waved her through.

It was on the tip of her tongue to say he wasn't invited. Yet how could she? He'd just invited her to accompany him on what promised to be a huge day in his life when hopefully Ben would be publicly accepted into his family—as long as that suspicious stepmother and her eldest behaved. If Ben had been pushy today…well, she could forgive him.

Truth to tell, she craved his company…as long as companionship didn't transgress into more heated waters. For a whole pile of reasons, sleeping together was on *big time indefinite delay*.

Back in the oversized boardroom, Ben tapped a glass with a spoon and addressed his audience. 'I have to leave for another appointment, but please stay and enjoy the refreshments. Thank you all for coming and sharing in the good news.'

After a burst of applause and raised glasses, the men went back to their conversations.

Ben returned to her side. 'If you want to say goodbye to your father I'll meet you in the lobby. Might save questions.'

She smiled. He'd read her mind.

Minutes later they met and walked to her shop,

which was only a block and a half through Sydney's CBD bustle.

'This new shop,' he said over the growling engine of a passing bus, 'it's for your flower business?'

Her brows knitted. 'A florist. And not just any florist. I have plans of becoming *the* place on the east coast for gift baskets and all floral requirements if your name happens to be Kidman or Murdoch.'

He nodded. 'Big plans.'

Was that a patronising quality to his tone? Sure, it was a big dream, but the only way to achieve big was to dream big. He of all people must understand that.

At the address, she unlocked the glass door, which led into a smallish space that was three parts fitted out in the same colours as her handbag store—pastel pink and vibrant blue with splashes of silver.

'Smaller orders will be done through here,' she told him with a gesture that encompassed the room. 'When we expand, I want to build or hire space at a more industrial-located estate.'

'To save costs on rental.'

She wove around the partition to check out the shelves and central working table out the back. 'The money and glamour needs to be where it can do its best work—in the arrangements. Working out an advertising schedule is next. Word of mouth in any industry is important too, so whatever comes out of here must be superior, unique and eye-catching without being gaudy...' She gave a crooked smile. 'Unless that's what the customer wants.'

She felt his eyes on her as she wandered around, checking electrical fittings, running a hand over the surfaces, ever vigilant of scratches or marks. When she'd given everything a mental tick, he smiled over at her. 'All set?'

'I'm happy.'

He took her hands and hot tingles sizzled up both arms. 'Good. Now we both have business out of the way, how about we go somewhere for a drink?'

She arched a wry brow. 'Like your place?'

He grinned. 'It is handy.'

Handy or fatal?

She wound her hands away from his. 'I think it's safer to see each other on Saturday.'

That would give her time to do the pregnancy test. See a doctor if she needed it confirmed. Figure out how to tell Ben he was going to be a father as well as how to duck the shrapnel after that.

He stepped into the space dividing them. 'Safe?' He frowned playfully. 'Come on. What happened to reckless?'

As he tipped forward she tipped back. 'Reckless has been packed up and sent on summer vacation.'

Reckless was what had got her into this mess. From the start she'd known he was dangerous. Dangerous for her heart.

'Pity. On Sunday I'd hoped we could take the boat out again.'

She recalled that day when he'd lavished her with his own spectacular style of attention and her stomach pitched. 'Let's get Saturday out of the way first.'

He narrowed one eye. 'Odd, but I don't get the sense you really want me to leave.'

She was burning up with longing, but, 'I can spell it for you?'

'And if I kiss you again?'

She backed up. He followed and her tail hit the counter. She swung an anxious look around his frame. 'You're aware there are streams of people filing by.'

'Suppose there weren't?'

She tried to steady her breathing. 'I'd still ask you to leave.'

He loomed nearer and her nipples tightened. His eyes crinkled above a smile. 'You would, huh?'

She tried to look unimpressed while covering the evidence by crossing her arms. 'What? So you're irresistible now?'

He lifted a brow. 'You tell me.'

Her arms unravelled as he came close enough for her to feel the heat radiating from his jacket... through the fabric of his trousers. Digging into her last reserves of determination, she composed her expression and shrugged.

'Ben Scott, you are absolutely *resistible*.'

His face lowered close to hers. Spice and musk filled her lungs, burrowed beneath her skin, throbbed through her veins. When his lips parted a hair's breadth from hers, a wonderful drugging pulse kicked off at her core. Lord, she was melting from the inside out.

'Do you remember that last time we were together?' he murmured, tilting his head so his warm breath mingled with hers. She quivered. Another millimetre and she could taste him again.

'Do you remember what you said?' he asked.

Her cheeks flamed. She remembered her words. She remembered how he hadn't hesitated to grant her wish. More than anything she remembered how it had felt every time he'd invented a new way to make her fly. Lord above, she was taking off only thinking about it, which was, no doubt, his plan.

His fingertip slid up and down the centre front of her skirt. 'Say it for me now.'

Her heart belted a mesmerising rhythm against her ribs. He was frying her brain. Crushing her strength.

'Ben,' she begged, 'people can see.'

'Just my back.'

Think, think!

'I heard a rumour you were a gentleman.'

That finger traced up as he nipped her bottom lip. 'Only if you want me to be.'

'Yes…' Her breath hitched. 'Please.'

His eyes drifted open and held hers for a heart-pounding moment. Slowly he eased back. Her legs almost buckled. A rag doll had more strength to stand.

He looked over his shoulder at the street, scrubbed his jaw and exhaled.

'You okay to lock up?' he finally asked.

She let out a breath and managed a convincing nod.

'You sure?' he insisted, and she nodded harder. 'Then I'll see you two o'clock Saturday.'

The self-assured look he sent as he left said today had been practice. Come Saturday he'd bring out his big guns.

CHAPTER EIGHT

APPLAUDING along with the rest of the wedding reception guests, Ben leaned towards Celeste, who looked breathtakingly elegant seated beside him.

'This should be the last of the speeches,' he let her know. 'Then we get to dance.'

Her big green eyes fixed on his and she gave a soft but slightly hesitant smile.

After leaving her in that shop on Monday, the hours until today had crawled by. It had been worth the wait. He hadn't had a more enjoyable day…being included in this special occasion, joining in a couple of professional family shots—not that Rhyll, his stepmother, or Paul, her eldest son, had approved.

He wouldn't let their loaded looks mar his pleasure, least of all being with Celeste again. Gorgeous in a shimmering lemon-coloured gown, she'd been the focus of his day. While she might still have reservations about *them*, she would also be the focus of his night.

All night.

At the bridal table, his brother Chris stood. Decked out in a black tie and dress shirt, his tux jacket draped over the back of his chair, he told a few stories, thanked his guests and kissed his blushing bride after announcing he would always remember how beautiful she looked today.

The applause died and Chris continued. 'Finally, 'I'd like to officially welcome another new member into our family. We had no idea our brother Ben was out there. I'm so happy you found us, mate.'

As Chris raised his glass Ben swallowed against the swell in his throat. Damn. He hadn't expected that, but he sure appreciated it.

Following etiquette, he half rose from his chair, bowed acknowledgement at Chris, then his father, who was seated at a nearby round table. Gerard's glass was raised, his blue eyes sparkling in the candelabra light. Ben returned the warm smile, then his gaze hooked on Rhyll. Setting her napkin on the table, she pushed to her feet and made a statement by walking calmly from the room.

Celeste's hand on Ben's sleeve helped him lower the rest of the way back into his seat.

While Chris cleared his throat and finished up, Ben tried to see his way clear to finding a solution to such an unfamiliar problem. He had no personal experience to draw upon, other than his long-established habit of reading the motivations of those around him. Rhyll was perhaps jealous of her husband's former love, Ben's mother, and anxious over how the appearance of a stranger-cum-son would impact upon her family, her marriage included. Paul felt his place as eldest son threatened and had let it be known that Ben was trespassing on his turf.

Ben had figured he could ignore the hostility, assume his usual place on the peripheral of a family dynamic and observe, but his gut told him that wasn't the answer this time.

Celeste laid a warm hand over his. 'I think they're playing our song.'

Brought back, he blinked across at her and the tune registered—the same song he'd played on the boat that night. He pushed back his chair. He'd never needed Celeste in his arms more than now, and, from the look in her eyes, she understood.

He led her out onto the timber floor and gathered her wonderful curves close. As their feet began to move in sync he gazed down into her eyes. 'Have I told you how incredible you look?'

Her lips twitched. 'Once or twice.'

'Not enough.' He twirled a finger around a golden lock. 'Is that glitter in your hair?'

'Just a sprinkle.'

He breathed in. 'And a new scent.' He arched a brow. 'You're definitely trying to drive me wild.'

Her brow creased. 'You're definitely trying to charm me.'

His mouth grazed her temple. 'Is it working?'

'And if I say no?'

'I'll be forced to show no mercy.'

He dipped her, Fred Astaire style. She shrieked out a laugh and he whirled her back up.

Her hair was a tassled mess. He loved it!

She blew out a breath, pushed back her hair, then tried to scowl. 'If you do that again, I'm sitting down.'

Two fingers ironed down the length of her spine, ending at the curve of her behind. Although she endeavoured to hide it, he felt her body respond, heating and coming alive against him.

He grinned. 'I have more subtle moves you might prefer.'

She sent a dry look. 'Is that supposed to be a surprise?'

'It's an invitation.'

She looked away and sighed. 'I know about your invitations.'

'That doesn't sound like a complaint.'

Her eyes challenged his. 'What do you want me to say? We're good in bed?' Her shoulders went up and down. 'All right. We're good in bed.'

The middle-aged couple dancing nearby sent them a curious look. Embarrassed, Celeste tucked herself against him.

Ben rolled back one shoulder. 'Well, now that's settled—'

'Nothing's settled.' She mumbled, 'Not yet.'

He caught her chin and lifted it. 'Running from each other won't fix things.' What they needed was to be together as they had been on his boat, and that amazing evening in his bed when the fireworks had gone off all night. 'You said it—we're good together.'

Her eyes glistened. 'Are we?'

He wanted to laugh—what a question! But he couldn't pretend to misunderstand her deeper meaning.

He danced her over to a quiet corner of the floor, then escorted her out onto a balcony. They stopped beside a giant trickling fountain of a marble cupid drawing his bow. When he kissed her fingertips and saw her nipples hardened beneath her bodice's sheer fabric, his tongue tingled in his mouth.

'We don't have to stay till the end,' he said. 'The formalities are over.'

'You don't want to stay for the party?'

'It was great being included in the day's events, but it might be wiser to leave this final hour or two to the Bartley-Scotts to enjoy free from the impostor.'

She squeezed his hand. 'Oh, Ben, I'm sure it will work itself out.'

He moved closer. 'Right now, all I'm worried about is you.' *Touching you. Kissing you. Making love with you.*

All. Night. Long.

Unable to hold off a moment more, his mouth took hers. When Celeste relented and dissolved against him, Ben cupped her nape and gave himself over to the intoxicating heavy thrum of his blood beating through all the parts of his body. Five weeks had been way too long. If he didn't take her soon, God save him, he might explode.

Their embrace was interrupted by a distant call.

'Two more love birds, I see.'

Recognising Gerard's voice, Ben reluctantly released Celeste. After shaking herself awake to her surroundings, she smoothed down the sides of her gown. Gerard was sauntering out into the brisk evening air, looking dapper, if not quite comfortable, in a full morning suit.

Getting his thoughts together, Ben inhaled deeply. 'It's been a great day, sir. Thanks for inviting us.'

Gerard stopped, a frown creasing the brow. 'I'm not a *sir*.' He clapped Ben's arm heartily. 'I'm your dad.' He gazed fondly at Celeste. 'You make a fine-looking couple.'

Ben smiled across. She was a fine-looking lady.

Gerard's expression turned solemn and he rubbed the back of his neck. 'Ben, son, I want to say I'm not unaware of my wife's and Paul's...*reluctance*.'

Ben waved a hand. He didn't want Gerard to feel bad. To be fair, it had been a shock for everyone involved.

'They'll come around,' Gerard assured him. 'There's no need to worry. You're part of my family now, no matter what.'

Ben nodded. That sounded good.

Maybe too good to be true.

Looking back at the reception doors, Gerard

seemed to gather himself. 'Marie'll make our Chris
a wonderful wife.'

Celeste agreed. 'She's lovely.'

Gerard tipped forward. 'She's the best cook.
Italian, you know. Do you cook, Celeste?'

'Only when I have to.' Celeste laughed. So did
Ben. Gerard took a moment, then joined them.

He nudged Ben. 'She's got a sense of humour. You
need that in a relationship.'

While Celeste lowered her gaze, Ben froze. They
weren't in a 'relationship'. Ben wasn't after a 'relationship'. They'd only seen each other a handful of
times. They were in a...well, an 'understanding'. Or
would be when he got Celeste back to his place and
they could reinstate what she'd said earlier. They
were 'good in bed'.

Stop the press. They were *great* in bed. Better
than great.

The music drifting out from inside changed and
Gerard exclaimed, 'I had the DJ play this song for
Rhyll. We danced to it the first night we met.' He
sighed. 'It goes so quickly. She has her ways, but I
can't imagine my life without her.'

As Gerard left his words echoed in Ben's mind.
She has her ways. Sounded as if there was a lot of
give and take in their marriage. Had to be, he
supposed, with bringing up seven children. He might
be worth millions, control the salaries of scores of
people, but Ben couldn't imagine the responsibility
that went with having a clutch of kids. The respon-

sibility of having even one, for that matter. He couldn't think of a thing that scared him…other than the infinite obligations associated with being a father.

A left-field thought struck.

Would he remember his and Celeste's song in thirty years' time?

Celeste began to move off too. 'Perhaps we should get back inside.'

He followed. 'Only to say goodbye.'

'And then?'

'I'm taking you home.'

She stopped and shook her head at the ground. 'I…I don't know.'

His hands sloped down her bare arms. 'I think you do.'

She searched his eyes for a long moment. 'You know what I really think? I think we need to talk.'

He held her eyes with his and nodded, then walked her inside. Certainly they could talk, as much as she wanted.

Over breakfast.

CHAPTER NINE

As THE lift glided up each floor to his apartment Celeste shrank a little more inside. Ben stood beside her, his big warm hand folded over hers. Every so often rocking back on his heels, he concentrated on the lift light, working its way higher.

Shaking inside, Celeste closed her eyes and tried to find her calm centre.

On the way home, she and Ben had kept the chatter light. But all the while she'd wondered, *Should I tell him? What will he say? We can't possibly make love. Will he even want to touch me when he knows?*

The lift pinged and he escorted her into the corridor. A moment later they were in his penthouse suite and all the memories of that New Year's night came rushing back—vivid, tingling. Dangerously, exquisitely hot.

He tossed his jacket over a chair back and moved to the bar. 'Can I get you a drink?'

'Water.' She trembled out a smile. 'Thanks.'

When he returned, she sipped while his chest

breathed in and out mere inches from her hand. As her heartbeat boomed in her ears she fought the urge to swipe the cool glass against her feverish brow.

Who was she kidding? He hadn't brought her here to talk. His agenda was seduction and she'd walked straight into his lair. What must he think other than the obvious? And, yes, she *did* want him to kiss her, just as she wanted his skilled hands all over her, threading through her hair, roaming over her naked limbs.

But she'd be better off running. They could 'talk' another day.

Decided, she thrust the glass towards him to take. 'I'm sorry. I've made a mistake.'

As his hand caught over hers on the glass his head angled and his brow creased with concern. 'Celeste? You're shaking.'

His jaw tight, he drew her over to the couch and, weak all over, she sank down alongside him.

'What's wrong?' he asked. 'This is more than nerves.'

When his finger carefully scooped hair from her brow behind her ear, she shivered at the contact.

Ben was an extraordinary specimen. Prime-time male in every way. Did that explain it—this gripping, uncontrollable thirst? But how could she allow herself to drink when she'd still be parched long after he'd grown tired of 'short term' and had moved on? If he'd known what she'd gone through…wondering if she'd conceived, buying that pregnancy kit, discovering the results—

His arm looped around her and he brought her close, obviously wanting to comfort her. His clean, musky scent worked its way into her lungs, through her system and, right or wrong, needing some kind of support, she leant more against him. As his palm lightly grazed her arm she dared to look up.

The golden light from the bar shone dimly. She could make out the strong planes of his face, the gleam of his eyes gazing down at her. How her fingers itched to trail along his shadowed jaw. Sample the soft bow of his lip...

He smiled softly. 'I know what you need.'

She knew too. A shrink.

He said, 'A relaxing massage.'

Tempting, but...

She let out a breath. 'I don't think that's it.'

He reached across and his right index finger and thumb scooped between her left ear and shoulder. Then he began to rub. Instantly a fleet of endorphins sailed out from the spot and waved a stream of soothing white flags.

Eyes drifting shut, she moaned as his touch gently rocked her.

Heaven.

She had to ask, 'Why have you never done this before?'

His lips brushed her brow as he spoke. 'I was saving it for a rainy day. Is that good?'

'You know it is,' she growled, but she only sounded satisfied.

'I can do better.'

He worked the area more fully until her bones melted away and her limbs began to float. She'd never had a professional massage; she'd doubted anything could measure up to even this tiny taste of Ben's manipulations.

Several drugging moments later, he turned more towards her, dotting soft, lingering kisses against her temple, then jaw. When his tongue grazed the seam of her lips, the sparking kindling deep inside her began to smoulder.

With great care, he tipped his body weight against hers. As her back met the couch cushions his fingers continued working her shoulder, but his mouth descended, tasting a provocative line down her décolletage.

With her eyes still closed, she told her brain to function through the blinding haze of passion. It refused. When he tugged her bodice down and his warm, wet mouth suctioned over the aching tip of her breast, brain function shut down completely. It was over.

She didn't want to resist.

As if sensing the precise moment of surrender, his hand left her shoulder and skied over her waist and hip, all the way down her leg until it caught her hem and dragged the fabric of her dress way up. His fingers hooked under her panties and slipped between her legs. As his fingertip delved between and gently rode her, and the stiff tip of his tongue twirled languidly around her nipple, her neck arced back and hips rose off the cushions. When his hand withdrew, in the far reaches of her mind she heard his fly unzip.

Felt the hot tip of him prod her thigh.

No!

Drunk with desire, she managed to push against his chest and drag herself to her senses. Summoning all her strength, she propelled herself upright and tried to steady her ragged breathing.

'*I can't do this.*'

His warm breath was at her ear. 'Celeste, honey, relax—'

'I won't relax. Ben, I said I wanted to *talk.*'

He straightened more and shovelled back dark hair flopped over his brow. He studied her, then he came closer. 'I'm sure that if—'

'I thought I was pregnant,' she rushed out, and felt better and worse for having admitted it.

His mouth dropped open. She thought she saw the blood drain from his face.

'You're…*pregnant*?'

She shook her head. 'I *thought* I was pregnant. Ended up…I wasn't.'

He simply stared at her. 'So you're not…having a baby?'

She hugged herself. 'Seems not.'

He slouched forward and his hands caught his head. 'Thank you, God.'

She flinched. Although she understood his relief,

after her recent roller coaster of emotional highs and lows, his reaction was a slap in the face. 'Well, it's great to see you're so happy about it.'

He stared as if her skin had turned purple. 'What's not to be relieved about?'

She held her chin firm. 'You have no empathy at all, do you?'

He frowned, genuinely puzzled. 'Empathy over what?'

Did she truly expect him to understand? To anyone who hadn't been in her place, it mightn't sound like much—*A bit late? Get over it.* But as Ben had once said...

'Guess you had to be there.'

His study of her cut her to the quick. 'Oh, I've been there. I was the product of an unplanned pregnancy, remember?'

Yes, she remembered, and she sympathised. But that was his experience. This had been hers.

She turned more towards him, needing to get it off her chest and for him to understand even a little.

'When I realised I was late, I was terrified. Then, as more days passed and the more I thought it over, I grew used to the idea and...' Remembered warmth filtered through her. She confessed, 'Well, I got excited. At the same time I felt this enormous crush of responsibility land on my shoulders. I bought a home pregnancy kit. Half of me wanted to know for sure, the other half simply didn't believe it.'

'The test was negative?' Her nod brought another groan of relief. 'Then that was it.'

She quashed her irritation. 'No, that wasn't it, because by that time I'd visualised the baby. The colour of his hair. How healthy she'd be. And I started to think about names, furniture—even schools. Once all those questions had done a few cycles, I was already committed to something that was physically half the size of a pea but that would grow into a baby.' *Her* baby.

She understood so well now.

When a woman had a child, that little person became their mother's number one priority. Women sacrificed. It was called 'maternal instinct'. Men didn't have it. They had 'slay and drag home the dinosaur' instinct; the human race was biologically designed that way for the survival of the species. He hunted, she nursed.

Her own mother had sacrificed. Anita had done what was needed in order to keep the family intact, which had meant rescuing her husband and his crumpling business, borrowing money that had never been repaid, then stepping away when Rodney had been able to capably take over. Her mother had never been thanked or acknowledged for any of it. In fact, as director of PLM, Rodney had had control over the funds, not Anita.

Even if Ben had been displeased at the 'baby situation', she'd known he would provide for them; she wouldn't *need* financial independence. But Celeste wanted it.

In these past days it had become crystal-clear how impotent her mother had felt the night she'd cried at Celeste's bedside. Powerless, defeated, committed to a man who might have respected her as a wife and mother, was happy to take money when she offered it, but resented his clever wife's threat to his masculinity. When Anita had died, she'd left her daughter that legacy.

Celeste never wanted to be 'looked after'.

She chewed her nail.

Ironic that Ben should have control of PLM now.

His voice deepened. 'Celeste, just so we're straight, I may not be ready for fatherhood, but there's no question that I would acknowledge my own child.'

She nodded. 'I know.'

He blinked at the floor and after a moment reached to hold her hand. 'I'm sorry.'

Her heart squeezed. She'd needed that.

She half shrugged. 'You didn't know.'

'But I was still responsible.'

Taking in his troubled face, she worried that she should have kept the false alarm to herself, but a bigger part of her was glad she hadn't. More often than not, a man didn't get to hear or appreciate the fear and doubt, or perhaps happiness and sense of purpose that followed a missed period; if Ben held such strong beliefs about parenthood he'd needed to hear it as much as she'd needed to share.

He kissed her hand. 'Feeling better about it now?'

She nodded, then thought more. 'Although, you'll probably think I'm silly, but the idea of going to Suzanne's baby shower next weekend has been driving me mad.'

'You're not looking forward to it?'

'She's a nice lady. I'm happy for her. The day's just going to be…awkward.' Because of how raw she felt over her own pregnancy misdiagnosis. Because the day would underpin the sense that she and Anita had been superseded.

'Would it help if I came along?'

She let his words sink in and brightened. 'You'd do that?'

He offered a crooked grin. 'As long as I don't have to diaper any dolls.'

She laughed. 'I'm sure we won't rope you in.'

His smile slowly faded. 'You want me to drive you home now?'

She considered it. Then, feeling stronger than she had in weeks, she leaned back against the bracket of his arm available behind her and said, 'Maybe soon.'

CHAPTER TEN

As THEY drove to her father's house the following Saturday Celeste drank in Ben's classic profile. Straight nose, strong bristled jaw, black hair and open white collar rumpling against the late summer breeze. Enthralled, she watched his tanned hands negotiate the sports wheel with such effortless precision.

Those hands worked magic.

However, after his massage and their discussion last weekend, she and Ben hadn't made love. He'd remained remarkably well behaved. They'd talked some more, then he'd driven her home. She'd thought constantly about him since. Although he'd started off commitment-phobic-minded when she'd confided in him about her *almost pregnant* dilemma, ultimately he seemed to appreciate at least some of what she'd gone through.

Better yet, he'd called every day this week, but hadn't hounded her. Because her story had scared him into holding back or because he'd discovered a new respect for her and their relationship, she couldn't be certain. Perhaps the shock idea of fatherhood had planted a positive and patient seed in his mind. Heck, he was here with her now, helping her to face this awkward day, wasn't he? Dared she hope?

Could Ben Scott be her Mr Right after all?

Discovering her study of him, he reached to clasp her hand. 'It'll be good to catch up with Rodney and give him an update on that meeting a couple of weeks back. I was on location yesterday. Helped dig a few post holes.' He smiled to himself. 'I still get a kick out of getting my hands dirty.'

Celeste clenched her teeth.

There it was…the stab she felt whenever he mentioned her family—

Sorry. What *had been* her family's company.

She looked away. 'I'm sure he'll be interested.'

Ben held her hand tighter as if he'd realised and regretted that, under the circumstances, his comment might have bit.

Facing her father today—with PLM sold and celebrating the baby's imminent arrival—seemed to sweep the past even farther behind them. Sometimes it was as if her mother—and that life—had never existed. She didn't blame Suzanne and she didn't want to blame her father, but sometimes… Well, sometimes it just plain hurt.

'You look all tight.' With one hand on the wheel, he massaged the sensitive sweep of her nearest shoulder. He grunted. 'Big knot right there.' His therapeutic yet sensual rub travelled up the back of her neck. 'How's that feel?'

She closed her eyes. 'Like I want you to do that to the rest of me.'

Her eyes sprang open.

Had she said that aloud?

'Careful,' he growled. 'I might pull over.'

Her skin grew hot at the thought. She was playing with fire. But maybe if she was very lucky she wouldn't end up being burned. Maybe this time instead of saying goodbye, she would finally find in Ben a wonderful warmth as well as a blistering passion.

His hand returned to the wheel as he turned into her father's street. 'If this is too hard, we don't have to go.'

She sat straighter. Suzanne had invited them for dinner, but Celeste knew it was wise not to push herself. People under stress sometimes said and did things they lived to regret. 'I said I'd go to the baby shower. We can say we have tickets to a play tonight.'

He didn't look convinced. 'Give me the nod when you're ready to leave.'

He pulled the Merc into the long driveway and Clancy and Matilda belted out from around the house. When Ben opened her car door, both dogs dropped their tennis balls at her feet.

Laughing, she ruffled their heads and picked up Clancy's ball. 'Wanna play, boy?'

The brown poodle wagged his tail so hard, he almost fell over.

She cast back, threw the ball and Clancy raced off. Matilda pranced around. When Celeste threw the second ball, it sailed through the air and lodged atop a bushy grevillea.

While Celeste cursed under her breath, Ben jogged off. 'I'll get it.'

Celeste waited for either her father to appear from the house or Ben to reappear from behind the bush. When neither showed up, she strolled off to see if she could help with the ball. Two pairs of eyes were better than one.

Ben was on his knees, searching under the bush. Matilda was sniffing and searching beside him.

Celeste examined the surrounding ground. 'Need any help?'

Ben's arms swept under the leaves. 'The ball's not stuck up the top. I figure it must have dropped.'

Her gaze lifted to the bush. Reaching into a branch, she pulled out the ball. 'Had your eyes tested lately?'

He peered up, frowned and grunted. 'Lucky find.'

She laughed. 'If you say so.'

His eyes flashed, then he caught her around the calves. She shrieked as she fell. Like a star footballer, he dived, rolled and somehow saved her from hitting the ground. With her lying on top of him— his arms locked around her trunk—he rolled again until she was pinned beneath him. He playfully manacled her hands either side of her head.

'Anything you want to say now, Miss Wise Guy?'

She found her breath. 'I hear horn-rimmed glasses are back.'

He chuckled. 'My eyes are just fine.' He squeezed her wrists. 'And they like what they see.'

She counted her heartbeats. 'What do they see?'

'Someone very special.' His gaze deepened. 'Someone I can't get out of my mind.'

Someone he'd want to marry?

His gaze narrowed as if he'd read her thoughts. Then he pushed up and helped her to her feet. 'We're expected. You'd better brush the grass off your skirt or tongues will wag.'

As they dusted off and walked back to the house Celeste couldn't help but wonder if she was a fool for setting herself up so easily for Ben's games. Or was she right in believing that since last weekend they'd finally made a real connection? That they were closer than they'd ever been to understanding each other?

Rodney descended the wide porch steps and greeted them. Her father brushed a kiss against her cheek, then took in her simple apricot to-the-ankles dress, her flowing hair.

'You look great, sweetheart.' He acknowledged Ben; Celeste had said he'd be joining her. 'Good to see you again, son.'

Ben took her father's hand. 'Rodney.'

'Hope you're taking care of my daughter as well as you're taking care of my business.'

Celeste cringed. Lord, she felt like a chattel. If

ghosts existed—if her mother could hear this conversation—

Her father's next words broke her train of thought. 'Suzanne's inside with her friends, unwrapping gifts and talking baby talk.' His gaze softened. 'She's pleased you came today.'

Celeste couldn't seem to fall over either side of the fence. Being here under these circumstances was like selling out her mother's memory, and yet the child Suzanne carried deserved a sister, just as Celeste deserved a sibling. No matter how much days like this hurt, she couldn't turn her back on that relationship.

Inside, hellos were exchanged between Celeste, Ben and half a dozen ogling women, who were clearly enamoured with his masculine looks and physique. When Suzanne enquired, Celeste replied that her handbag store was doing a roaring trade and her florist concern—Star Arrangements—was a week away from opening its doors. When a lady in a pink silk lounge suit suggested she bring out the food, Celeste offered instead. Rodney had taken a phone call, so Ben said he would help.

In the kitchen, he collected a silver tray of ribbon sandwiches.

An image bloomed in her mind and, grinning, Celeste leant against the counter. 'What's the bet those women would love to see you serve them minus your shirt.'

He looked surprised, then gave her a devilish grin. 'I'm only available for private shows.'

As she remembered the blood-pumping feel of his bare, hot chest against her flesh her heart began to race. She fought the impulse to gravitate towards him and shook her head instead. 'Not today.'

'How about tonight?'

She wouldn't lie to herself and say she wasn't interested. And whether it was emotional suicide or not, she couldn't help but have some fun with his quip.

As he sauntered nearer she made an observation. 'You look hungry. Here. Have some dip.' She shoved a cracker in his mouth.

The surprise faded from his face as he chewed and mumbled, 'Thank you. Delicious.' He set down his tray. 'Now perhaps I could tempt you with something tasty. Do you prefer spicy—' he indicated fatty Mexican meatballs '—or sweet?' Scones and cream.

Smothering a grin, she turned to collect her own tray. 'I like a healthy diet.'

He caught her waist. 'I like you.'

As his mouth hovered close to hers the air hummed and throbbed between them. It was all she could do not to succumb to temptation and allow herself to be kissed. Every particle of her screamed out to give in.

But it wasn't the time or the place.

More than that…was it wise?

Summoning her will power, she ducked under his arm and scooped up her tray. 'Suzanne would like to start her shower.'

After delivering his tray, Ben bowed off and joined Rodney in his study. Gathering herself after their steamy interlude in the kitchen, Celeste sat next to a chatty lady on the twin couch and watched Suzanne fawn over beautifully crafted matinee jackets, cot mobiles, rattles, baby's first fine bone china…

When Suzanne unwrapped Celeste's gift, her eyes filled. Overcome, she moved closer. Celeste stood so she could accept her stepmother's hug and kiss.

'It's a perfect gift,' Suzanne, smelling of 'Joy', murmured at her ear. 'Thank you.'

Pleased that she liked it, Celeste showed her the bag's many compartments. 'It might look like a big teddy bear but it's very practical. The head fits all your bottle needs, the tummy is for diapers. Its back pouch is for lotions and such. The front pouch for food.'

'Where did you get it?' Miss Chatty with the black bob asked over her Royal Doulton cup.

'I designed it and had a seamstress do the work.' She indicated the bear's tummy. 'See. *Celeste's*.' Then a trademark silver star.

As the women spoke up, each desperate to make an order, without warning, Celeste's throat constricted. She'd thought of this design during *that* week.

The test had shown she wasn't pregnant. It was silly to be upset. It was only this environment— clucky women, some of them pregnant—that had brought all those empty emotions back home.

Suzanne held the teddy baby bag to her belly. 'It's

a wonderful gift. I'd always wanted children. I'm so happy it's happened now and she'll have such a special sister.'

Suzanne was being genuinely kind, but right now Celeste felt as if she might suffocate.

Mrs Perfectly Poised with the blonde chignon bit into a jam and cream scone and licked her thumb. 'Did you bake this, Suzanne? Your scones are always lighter than air.'

'It's all in the oven temperature.' Suzanne crossed to retrieve her cup from a polished timber trolley. She exercised her back and her pregnant tummy stuck out more. 'It needs to be *very* hot.'

Celeste raised her brows. Her mother had taught her nothing about cooking. Instead she'd passed on her love for watercolours and horse riding. Celeste remembered her father being cross one morning when he'd needed to iron his own shirt. Had that been after Anita had acquired that loan from Grandpa, or a night when she'd been up until three stringing together strategies to pull PLM out of the hole her husband had dug?

Suzanne wouldn't need to iron any shirts. Those struggles were over, fought and won by another.

Brushing back her hair, Celeste tried to breathe. She needed air. Or, more simply, she needed to get out of here.

Ben materialised at the right moment, looking darkly attractive and capable as ever. She begged him with her eyes.

He checked the time and commented to Rodney, who was a step behind, 'We must be going. Tickets to the theatre.'

He mentioned the name of the play and all the women swooned. They said goodbye on the porch and everyone, including Miss Chatty and Mrs Poise, waved them off.

When they were a mile down the road, Ben pulled over. He ratcheted up the handbrake, cupped his palm around her nape and dragged her close. His kiss had the detonating accuracy of a precision missile. It left her completely shattered and buzzing with a high-powered sexual need as well as a promise of what was yet to come...*if* she were brave or stupid enough to accept.

Too soon, his lips left hers. He growled in his throat. 'I've been dying to do that all day.'

She wouldn't admit that she'd been just as desperate. Her body felt alight with sizzling want and need. What would happen when they reached home? Probably not much talking. But the same question haunted her. As an affirmed bachelor, would Ben ever want more from her than casual companionship and sex?

Ben released her and, after checking the rear view mirror, pulled back out onto the deserted road. After a few moments he asked, 'Did you have a nice time?'

She conceded, 'It wasn't all bad.'

'Suzanne looked very pregnant today.'

'She hasn't got long to go.'

'She seemed happy. Rodney too.'

'Most couples do in the beginning.' She cringed. 'That wasn't nice.'

'It'll take time to get used to seeing your dad with someone else. Don't feel bad.'

'Suzanne's so friendly and sincere. She doesn't deserve snarky comments like that.'

'She's just the kind of woman Rodney needs in his later years.'

She blinked over at him. 'What kind of woman is that?'

She could make out his expression. *Foot in mouth.* 'That wasn't meant to be a slur against your mother.'

She tried to smile. 'That's all right. What kind of woman did you mean? Attractive? Thoughtful? A woman who'll be content to stay home and look after the baby while he plays nine holes?'

He scratched his temple. 'I didn't say that.'

'Suzanne is lovely—' she made that clear again '—but not everyone wants to stay home and look after babies. Nothing against those who do, coz I hear it's the hardest job in the world as well as the most rewarding.' She thought of her mother and herself. 'But some of us want to explore our options and keep them open alongside marriage and motherhood. It's not a crime.'

Or not in most countries.

'I'm not suggesting women shouldn't have careers. But you must admit it's logical that if a couple choose to have a family, given that women are the main care givers, they need to put things on hold. That's what the paid maternity leave ruckus is about, isn't it?'

Celeste pulled on her seat-belt sash.

Ruckus?

She turned more towards him. 'Why does a woman have to be the one to step down?'

He seemed amused. 'Not step down. Delay.'

'Because the family might suffer if she's not home to mash the spuds?'

She remembered how pleased Gerard had been that Chris's new bride was a ten in the kitchen, and how her own father had subtly criticised her mother's cooking. Celeste had thought her mother's failed attempts at sponge cake were good fun. They got covered in flour and she was always allowed to lick the spoon. And if ever Anita burned the roast, it simply meant more dessert. Who could complain?

'Celeste, you know I can cook.'

'Very well. But you're avoiding the question.'

He lifted a brow. 'You *are* after an argument.'

She almost laughed. 'Because I want to discuss equality of the sexes.'

His face hardened. 'It's not about equality. It's simply the way the world works.'

Her chest burned with indignation. 'Your world or mine?'

He clenched his jaw—a warning to drop it—but she couldn't let it rest there.

'These days there are men who stay at home to look after the baby while a mother works.'

While she high-fived that initiative if it suited the couple concerned, Celeste didn't feel that was her answer. She dearly wanted to nurse and care for her own baby when it was time. She simply didn't want to relinquish her individual power as a consequence. Wasn't that fair enough?

She turned the tables. 'Would you be prepared to delay your goals and be dependent on another person?'

'I was dependent enough on others the first sixteen years of my life.'

As she thought of the sad little boy he once must have been her heart dropped. However. 'I wasn't responsible for your past. Right now I'm concerned with the future.'

'I've pretty much accomplished my goals.'

'Like being boss of a company like PLM?'

He turned at her tone. 'You knew how I felt about PLM from the start. I can't change my story now.'

'And I can't change mine.'

Her mother had sacrificed everything and someone called Benton Scott—the man who had become her lover—had ended up with the prize. Sometimes she couldn't believe that twist of fate. It wasn't Ben's fault, but, truth was, it still stuck in her craw.

His expression softened. 'You're much better off with your florist concern. It'll be huge, and you know I'll help anyway I can.'

Another brick went up. Why did he think he could decide what was best for her? 'I don't want your help.'

She didn't want *anyone's* help—not her father's

any more, and not Ben's. She wanted to do it her way, just as Ben had done for himself, and would continue to do.

His mouth hooked up at one side but she saw the muscle jump in his jaw. 'You could make a guy think his help isn't good enough.'

Her chin pulled in. 'That's not it.'

He kept his gaze on the road as if she might read too much from his eyes.

'Are you sure?' he asked. 'You were born with a silver spoon in your mouth. I'm the penniless orphan with no pedigree who clawed his way up from the gutter.'

What? 'Why would you say something like that?'

'Because your father wasn't good enough for your mother.'

She blinked several times. 'What's that supposed to mean?'

'If he had been, she wouldn't have tried to make him into something he wasn't. Hell, maybe the guy was sincerely happy fixing mowers. Maybe she should've let him be the man he wanted to be and—'

Stunned, she waited. 'And what?'

He changed gears. 'And nothing.'

She said it for him. 'And their marriage would've been more of a success? Rodney didn't have to take my grandfather's money, you know.'

Ben coughed out a humourless laugh. '*Didn't he?* I can feel the pressure on him now and it happened twenty years ago. You said it yourself. Your mother usually won the toss and your father grew to resent it.'

Her mouth dropped open. 'So a woman should hide her intelligence? Never aspire to achieve?'

But somewhere deep inside a young girl whispered, *I just want Mummy and Daddy to love each other again.*

Which meant what? Mummy had to sell her soul to keep the peace?

Ben scrubbed his jaw and spoke more calmly. 'You should never need to worry like your mother did. While we're together, you'll always have the best. I don't want you to be concerned over money matters.'

While they were together? And how long would that be?

She felt torn for another reason. 'That sounds sweet on the surface, but it equates to being kept in the dark. Would you take me seriously if I suggested that to you?'

He looked at her as if she might be coming down with something.

Darn it, she wanted answers. But were there any?

She couldn't run from it any longer. She'd fallen in love with the very man who had exploded into her life three months earlier and had unwittingly taken what had amounted to her right to see her mother's memory, and last wish, honoured. Ben sympathised over how the deal had worked out. But could he ever appreciate how she felt—not only about that specific issue, but also the broader issues?

She'd wanted to put the past behind her, but maybe she shouldn't because she was loath to repeat her mother's mistakes and Ben's attitude set off alarms. Clearly he thought a woman's—or at least a mother's—place was primarily in the home, and a man should be allowed 'to do what a man needed to do'. She, on the other hand, advocated individuality and equality between the sexes in all things. He had trouble seeing her point; she had to wonder, given his childhood of wishing for a textbook family, if he was even capable.

'You know what's wrong with this discussion?' she finally asked. 'That you should want to come off sounding like such an expert on a subject you otherwise avoid like the plague.' Marriage.

'I'm entitled to my opinion.'

'Based on what? You cling to these idealised notions of how a family should work.' The man as head of the house, the woman happily keeping her place in the bedroom and kitchen. 'You want to preach about the way a couple should be content and stick together as a family, yet you don't have the guts to go for it yourself.'

He edged over a patronising look. 'Celeste, we only met three months ago.'

'Are you telling me that in the future you'd consider long term? That you'd no longer view *us* as a romp, or me as someone you won't commit to beyond the bedroom?'

His face hardened and hands tightened on the wheel.

Her chest ached. She crossed her arms and looked out the window. 'I didn't think so.' So full of wisdom, but not prepared to put his own heart on the line.

Must be high time she withdrew her own heart as well.

He swerved into a park outside her apartment building. She opened her door at the same time his door unlatched.

His leg was already out the door. 'I'm coming up.'

She spun on him. 'No, Ben, you're not. This ends now. Maybe happy families isn't a matter of waving a magic wand or wishing on a star. I know that as well as you do. But one day I hope to find the man I'm meant to spend the rest of my life with. Though I would've liked it to be you, for so many reasons it's obviously not. Aside from sexual attraction, we started off miles apart and I can't ever see that rift closing.'

He reached for her hand, but she pulled away as her throat clogged with emotion. She bit her lip, then lifted her chin. 'I don't want to do this any more. Don't call. You have the company, you have my heart, but I'll get over it. I'll get over you—if you have the decency to stay away.'

She needed to get on with her life—find her place—and this was only delaying it.

She shut the car door behind her—made it all the way up to her apartment. Then reality hit, pain overwhelmed her and stinging tears began to flow.

CHAPTER ELEVEN

COULD things get any worse?

Gerard's voice on the phone this morning had suggested the family matter was urgent. But after the disastrous end to his outing with Celeste, Ben felt more like donning his track shoes and running out his frustrations till he dropped than attending a Bartley-Scott family meeting.

He wasn't good at collaborating with others on family politics. Hadn't Celeste slammed home that point so well before she'd strode away yesterday? But today Ben felt stuck. After the way his father had welcomed him into his fold, Ben didn't want to refuse Gerard's invitation to his home—although Ben sensed he alone was the reason for the gathering.

As Ben walked into the Bartley-Scott kitchen his misgivings seemed to be confirmed when two pair of eyes out of a dozen glared up at his arrival. Ben's irritation, as well as another emotion he wouldn't name, spiked into the red. Hell, you'd think he'd killed someone.

Gerard indicated a chair. 'Take a seat, Ben. You're the last to arrive.'

Ben shucked back his shoulders. 'I prefer to stand, thank you.'

Since his earliest memories, he'd dreamed of finding his family, being accepted. But the cold facts of reality weren't that shiny or clear, and, like nothing else could, it made him want to run.

Maybe Celeste was right. All his life he'd relied on no one but himself. Maybe he would always come up short when it came to taking that final leap—being able to commit totally. Trust wasn't easy to come by.

Zack, Paul's young son, scooted up and tugged Ben's trouser leg. 'Where's C'leste? She was at the wedding.'

Ben ignored the emotional kick in his gut. 'She couldn't come today.'

Gerard patted Zack's shoulder. 'Can you go out the back to play for a few minutes? Grandpa needs to talk to the adults.'

'Will Ben be here when I get back?' Zack spoke under his breath, 'Daddy doesn't like him so much.'

Paul shot up from his chair. 'Zack!'

Ben suppressed a groan. Nothing could be worth this. He'd felt like the whipping boy for the first half of his life; what the hell was he doing here feeling uncomfortable when he could go back to feeling…

Nothing.

Gerard ruffled his grandson's hair. 'Run along. Daddy'll go fetch you when we're done.'

After the back screen door closed, Gerard moved to stand at the head of the table. His seven children—eight including Ben—waited for his next words. Rhyll sat by a window, head down, busy darning a sock.

Gerard called her over. 'Rhyll, put down that needle and thread and come stand beside me.'

Reluctantly she set down her work and joined her husband.

Gerard leant forward, his two palms on the table. 'It's sometimes difficult to know how to handle family situations. They come along a lot—disagreements, discipline issues, agreeing on whose turn it is to take out the garbage.'

Ben crossed his arms. He hoped that wasn't a subtle reference.

Gerard continued. 'No one's missed the vibes generated toward Ben. Most are welcoming, but some…' His face twisted and he pulled up tall. 'Well, some are disappointing if, perhaps, understandable. I'd initially thought I should let the waters calm by themselves, but Ben deserves more than that. And so…' He turned to his wife.

Before he could speak, Rhyll's face coloured and she stepped back. 'I don't think there's a need to talk in front of the—'

Gerard held up a hand. 'There's a *big* need.' He took both her hands in his. 'Yes, I was married before, but I assure you that I didn't see Ben's mother again after that final night when Ben was obviously conceived. I have never been unfaithful to you. Never will. You are my wife and will be till the day I die. My family is the most important thing in the world to me. I know this uncertainty is partly my fault. I should remind you of my feelings more often.'

While Ben blinked at Gerard's unadorned honesty, Rhyll seemed to hold her breath, then her shoulders came down and she smiled.

Gerard pressed a loving kiss to her cheek and turned to Paul, who sat up straighter. 'You are my firstborn. The baby boy I held in my arms and was so proud of. Still am. But I've been given a gift most men could never hope for. *Another* firstborn, and I won't turn my back on him for anything, just as you will never turn your back on Zack. Paul, I spoke to you constantly about Ben when I first found out, about how successful he was, how he'd built himself up from nothing. I didn't mean to make you feel uncertain of your place in my heart. You could never be replaced, but just as you hope that Zack will one day have a brother or sister, you need to understand that we, as a family, have been blessed in the same wonderful way.' His next words addressed the whole room. 'Life's never long enough. Let's all spend it making up for lost time, starting now.'

Everyone's eyes fell to Paul. Paul's jaw flexed, then his gaze drifted towards the screen door, to the backyard where his son played. His young wife touched his hand. He nodded, pushed out his chair and walked over to Ben. Nodding, he stuck out his hand.

His throat aching, Ben exhaled and accepted his younger brother's olive branch.

Paul grinned. 'Guess the last couple of weeks make up for all the spats we missed out on growing up. A little late but—' Paul brought Ben close for a brotherly hug '—sorry for being an idiot. Welcome to the family.'

Her face contrite, Rhyll came forward. 'Can I get you a cup of tea, Ben? I baked some banana bread this morning. It's always been the kids' favourite.'

Melissa, Dana and Belinda, Ben's three half-sisters, chirped up to agree. Paul's wife, Chris and Marie moved over towards Ben too, while Michael and Terrance, Ben's youngest siblings, swiped some banana bread off the table.

Gerard waved a beckoning hand. 'Ben, when you're ready, will you join me on the back porch?'

Ben's mind was spinning. He'd witnessed foster dads address their families, however—other than that one time when he'd briefly felt included—he'd hovered on the outside. He'd never felt connected.

Or loved.

Until now.

He and Gerard moved out onto the back porch and sat on the back steps side by side, watching Zack ride his bike minus trainer wheels.

Ben spoke first. 'Thank you.' Simple words, but heartfelt.

Gerard smiled. 'I hope you'll come by often. With seven…sorry, *eight* children, the fun never ends, even when they're all grown up. But you'll know about that one day yourself.'

Ben watched Zack and his bike weave around.

Would he know one day? Three months ago becoming a father had been the farthermost thing from his mind. Celeste's pregnancy alarm the other week had been an eye-opener. But he'd still baulked at seeing himself in what he'd perceived as a scary role. Marriage. Kids.

Ben frowned. He needed to know. 'What was my mother like?'

Gerard inhaled deeply. 'She was a good woman, who felt strongly about her independence and opinions. Not a thing wrong with that. I admired her courage.' He shrugged. 'We just weren't meant to be.'

Ben read between the lines.

'You didn't see eye to eye.' Like Celeste and himself at times.

'Ben, your mother and I thought we were in love. We made a mistake. But even Rhyll and I—in fact, in any marriage a husband and wife aren't going to agree on everything. It's simply not possible. It's how you deal with those issues that will help make a family solid and endure.'

Ben had witnessed that sound advice in action first-hand today. Being a good father wasn't easy. It was a responsibility to be handled with great care and deep consideration. It meant bridging disagreements as well as admitting to your own mistakes. Admitting to your feelings. Having the guts to say I love you to the people—the person—who mattered most…

And doing it before it was too late.

CHAPTER TWELVE

CELESTE glanced up from her Star Arrangements counter and felt her heart leap from her chest. Her pen clattered to the floor as she tried to catch her stolen breath.

'Ben…what are you doing here?'

He sauntered up, his gaze dark and penetrating as if he'd walked a thousand miles and nothing could shake his resolve. 'I need to speak with you.'

She came out from behind the counter. 'I told you two days ago…' Her stomach muscles gripped but she said it anyway. 'I need you to stay away.'

His voice lowered. 'I can't, and I don't think you want me to either.'

The conviction in his eyes…the temptation of his suggestion…

She found the strength to turn away. She couldn't survive another round battling Ben's magnetism.

'What I *want* doesn't count. I'm concerned with what I need.' What was *best*, which was to put their affair from her mind and down to experience.

She couldn't regret the time she'd spent with Ben; what woman could? But on Saturday he'd made it clear: their relationship was going nowhere. If she relented now, she was as good as telling him she was prepared to be his mistress. It was an old-fashioned term, but well suited the situation he obviously preferred. No ties. No hassles. Just good times, including very good sex. But, she'd learned, sometimes good sex had big consequences.

His hands cupped her shoulders. A tingling moment later, his warm breath stirred her hair. 'I spent some soul-searching time with my family yesterday and I've come to a decision. You need me, Celeste. And I need you.'

Soul-searching?

She set her teeth and shrugged away to face him. 'Here's a newsflash, Ben. Sex isn't everything.'

'I'm not talking about sex.' He ran a hand through his hair. 'Well, not *only* sex.'

She huffed. Nothing had changed.

She lifted her chin at the door. 'Please leave. I'm opening the store next week and I'm busy tying up loose ends.'

She needed to concentrate her efforts here—on her business and building her own niche in the world, not wasting time vacillating over a silver-tongued playboy who had all the answers but wasn't interested in putting his heart where his mouth was.

'Celeste, I've thought a lot about us. I've had no

sleep these past days, going over every aspect of our relationship.'

Her hands curled at her sides. 'We don't have a relationship.'

He ignored that. 'And I kept coming back with the same answer. I want long term. I want to marry you.' He shrugged and smiled. 'It's that simple.'

The cogs in Celeste's brain seized as every element of time seemed to screech to a halt. She waited for the brackets to form around that oh-so-kissable mouth. But he didn't grin.

This wasn't a joke?

But a proposal from a man who two days ago had shuddered at the prospect of settling down, even while dictating how it should be done? It didn't fit.

Unless…

The chain mail went back up around her emotions. She shook her head. 'It won't work.'

He frowned. 'What won't work?'

'A fake engagement that's designed to get me back beneath your sheets.'

His brow creased more. He was a good actor—good enough to appear as if her suggestion had stung. 'That's not it.'

Wasn't it? When had he said that he loved her? She'd have thought those words would play an important role when a man asked a woman to spend the rest of her life with him. If he'd thought so hard about this, where was the ring? This was clearly a scam, Benton Scott digging extra deep to work his ticket into her bedroom. Well, sorry, but that train had left the station.

She crossed her arms over the empty ache expanding beneath her ribs and arched a brow. 'So you've had some kind of revelation?'

His head cocked. 'If you want to call it that.'

She called *it* something else.

Seduction.

She wouldn't go there again. 'Sorry, but I'm not convinced.'

He moved towards her, his arms out. 'Celeste—'

She shot her arms out too, but warning him away. 'I asked you to leave me alone.' Her voice cracked. 'Can't you respect me that much?' He was breaking her heart all over again. She'd had her hopes raised before. She didn't need to have them crushed still more.

He held her gaze for a heart-rending moment, then he pushed out a breath. 'I need to admit you were right. I had this vision of what a family should be, but I was too much of a coward to test the theory. And part of the reason was that I knew I would never find my perfect *home-sweet-home* package. But yesterday I learned that I don't need perfection. I need to work every day on what means more to me than anything.'

He was referring to her?

She wound her arms tighter. She would not be swayed by his entrancing blue eyes and deadly brand of charm. 'I can think of at least one thing that means more to you than me.'

'PLM?' She nodded. He handed over a large envelope he'd been carrying.

She flipped it over. 'What's this?'

'Documents to release the proprietorship of PLM into your name.'

Her eyes narrowed. 'Is this some kind of joke?'

'I won't pretend it wasn't great fun…to own that company…to be a boy but be in charge. But PLM will always be far more than that to you.'

Her heart pounded high in her throat.

He couldn't be serious.

This wasn't right.

She shoved the envelope back. 'I can't accept this.'

He shook his head slowly. 'Take it, even if you eventually find you want to sell it again.'

She swallowed hard, trying to make sense of it all. 'But this must be worth…well, at least the debt you paid.'

'Money isn't the issue.'

He'd told her he wanted to marry her. Now he was handing back something that had meant so much to both of them: to her because it had encompassed where she'd come from and who she'd thought she needed to be, and to Ben because when a person hadn't been given love, they naturally sought out some other source of power. More than anything, PLM had represented power over his lost childhood. Now he was giving that power up.

For her.

Her tongue was still tied when he dropped a kiss on her brow. 'Take it,' he murmured. 'It was never mine.'

As he turned to leave her cell phone rang and he turned back. 'You should get that. Could be your first big Star Arrangements client.'

Right now—with her mind in turmoil—she didn't care if it was.

He concentrated on her, then on the phone ringing on the counter. He moved to collect it and handed it over.

Her rubber lips worked enough to say hello. When she hung up a few seconds later, the world seemed to have tilted. She dropped the envelope as her legs threatened to collapse beneath her. She heard Ben's voice, though distantly.

'Celeste? What's wrong?'

She touched her clammy forehead. 'Suzanne had the baby but she's haemorrhaging. I've never heard Dad sound like that before.' Thick with unshed tears. But she *had* heard him like that—when her mother had passed away.

Ben secured her cold hands in his. 'Which hospital?'

She dug through the fog and came up with a name. He grabbed her purse off the counter and ushered her out the door, through the busy city pedestrian traffic and into his building's underground car park.

By the time they were in the car and on their way, Celeste had settled enough to explain. 'The baby's fine but Suzanne's in a bad way. The doctor's examined her. She's on medication to help stem the bleeding. But her vital signs are far from stable. If it doesn't stop, she'll need a transfusion.'

And surgery if the situation didn't improve. Celeste didn't want to think beyond that and yet she couldn't help but worry about that new tiny baby— her own little sister—growing up without her mum as she had done from the age of ten. As she held her knotting stomach another thought struck. She fixed her eyes on Ben, whose face was more set than she'd ever seen.

He was here for her; he obviously wanted Suzanne well, but surely he was pondering the fact that he'd lost his mother in similar circumstances.

He reached for her hand and shot her a determined smile. 'She'll be fine.'

Her chest grew warm. She'd never felt closer to him than at this moment. He was a man anyone could rely on in an emergency to keep his head and get everyone through. She knew that as well as she knew her own name. And he'd said he wanted to marry her and had proven it the best way he knew how. By giving her back her past.

But what of their future?

Her free hand gripped in her lap as she took in his strong profile.

Was he sexist? Was she too much the feminist? Was theirs a volatile and ultimately toxic combination? Or could there be a compromise on their thinking?

When they entered the hospital ward, a nurse at the station let them know which room.

They fast-tracked it down the corridor and into the private maternity suite. Suzanne lay asleep—or unconscious—in a crisply made bed, a drip in her arm. Rodney sat in a chair beside her, holding close a small wrapped bundle.

He looked up as they entered and his suntanned face beamed. 'Sweetheart, you're here.'

She felt Ben's arm steadying her, but she didn't dare speak. Was Suzanne any better? Had she had a transfusion? Gazing down again at his new little daughter, her father appeared relaxed.

Suzanne's heavy eyes opened. She wet her lips and attempted a smile. 'Here's big sister.'

Her heart belting against her ribs, Celeste moved closer. 'I thought… Dad, you said…'

Her father groaned on a nod. 'I shouldn't have phoned when I did. It was a scary time. I'm sorry now that I worried you. Suzanne was wheeled back in ten minutes ago. The doctor's happy with how she's responded to the medication.'

Her face pale but content, Suzanne took in her family—husband and child. 'I wasn't worried. We have the best obstetrician in Sydney. And the baby's healthy. She cried almost the second she was delivered.'

Celeste smiled, then felt a flicker of disloyalty that she was happy this woman was alive when her own mother was dead. But that, she realised fully, wasn't the way it should be. She had wonderful memories of her mother. And now she had a thoughtful step-mother, who wanted them all to be a family. She also had a father who had his faults, but loved her nonetheless and deserved a second chance as much as anyone.

And what about this new addition?

Celeste drifted towards the bundle in her father's arms. She gazed down and her heart brimmed with immediate unconditional love.

She swallowed against rising emotion. 'She's so tiny. And *beautiful*.' Delicate rosebud mouth…jet-black hair and lashes…bunched above the wrap, fingers that were so small and perfect, each and every one was a miracle.

Rodney nodded. 'I think she looks a little like you.'

'Same nose,' Suzanne offered.

Celeste remembered the week when she'd wondered if she was pregnant. She laid a hand atop this sleeping baby's head and knew when the time was right, it would happen.

'We named her Tiegan,' her father said. 'It means little princess.'

Ben's low voice rumbled behind Celeste. 'Every girl deserves to be a princess. Congratulations.'

Celeste looked over her shoulder and let her gaze roam Ben's face—his genuine smile as well as the faint line drawn between the dark slashes of his brows. Seeming to convey some message with his eyes, he reached to take her hands and press his lips to each one.

'Want a hold?'

Her father's offer brought Celeste back. Nodding, she positioned herself in a comfortable chair. Her father stood and carefully placed the baby in her arms.

A rush of wonderment had Celeste muffling a laugh. The baby was so real and warm and somehow heavier than she'd expected. 'I thought she'd be lighter.'

'Like the dolls you used to carry around.'

She studied her father. 'You remember?'

Chuckling, he sat on the bed and laid his hand over his wife's. 'You were doll crazy. Every Christmas, every birthday, you only wanted to add to your collection. Your mother and I would joke you'd have twelve children some day.'

Suzanne smiled. 'There's still time.'

Twelve children! Celeste wanted to hoot, but the moment was too special…the kind of moment a person remembered and treasured for ever. Then she knew.

She didn't need to be visible or prove herself in her father's, or anyone's, world any more. She simply wanted to share and be a part of it. Of this.

'Does this mean we have a babysitter?' Rodney asked.

Tiegan yawned and Celeste's heart melted more. 'Whenever you need me, I'll be there.'

It might've been all the emotion in the room, but didn't it follow that if she'd found her way here—to a place where she could wholeheartedly accept this new phase in her life—maybe she could accept a little more? Should she give Ben the benefit of the doubt just one more time? Would it be foolhardy, or her own chance to find lasting happiness?

She looked up from the baby's peaceful face, searched the room, then frowned. 'Where's Ben?'

Her father threw a glance around; Suzanne opened her eyes and blinked into the corners too.

'He's probably popped out for some air,' Rodney decided.

Without saying a word?

Celeste swallowed the dread creeping up her throat.

She had another theory. Having understood that everything was squared away here—including her relationship with the baby, Suzanne and her father— Ben had ducked out quietly without putting her through yet another goodbye.

Should she go after him?

She blew out a breath. 'Dad, can you take Tiegan?'

'Sure, sweetheart.'

He scooped the baby up and Celeste headed for the door. 'I'm sorry. I have to go.'

'Go where?'

She was halfway out. 'Hopefully home.'

While her father looked at her oddly, Suzanne's smile said she understood.

Celeste passed the unattended station, then came across a nurse checking a chart. 'Did you see a very tall, very good looking man pass by here?'

The nurse grinned. 'Did I ever.' She pointed her Bic at the lifts. 'He went down.'

When Celeste jumped out of the lift a few moments later and made her way outside, the air had turned unseasonably cool. The nippy air wrapped around her shoulders and inched up her skirt. She hunched, then rubbed her hands. She wished she'd brought a jacket. She'd always kept one in Ben's car—

Her focus honed in on the car park. His Mercedes was zooming off down the road.

Her hand shot up as she called out, 'Ben!'

Celeste's hand slowly lowered.

He was gone. But should she have expected anything more? He'd told her that he wanted to marry her and she'd said she didn't believe him. And yet he'd still acted to get her here in record time. Without making a scene, he'd kissed her hands and had said a final goodbye. Should she leave it at that? Would she only be opening a tin of worms to want to see him again?

With a thousand questions buzzing through her brain and her heart thudding low in her chest, she dragged herself around to face the hospital entrance. But Suzanne must need rest, and her father would want time on his own with baby Tiegan—it was only natural.

So…where to now?

Hugging her chilled arms, she walked aimlessly down the path, along a back street and eventually came across a field, set up with a lively long weekend carnival. A slow spinning Ferris wheel, enthralled children on merry-go-rounds, a juggling clown with baggy striped pants riding a unicycle and tooting a horn…

She wandered in, waving off a man who offered five balls to knock down the cans and win a giant doll. She couldn't throw for peanuts. But she wouldn't tell Ben that.

Her eyes misted over.

She'd missed him so much. Now she felt that sense of loneliness like a hot lance through her heart. What should she do?

'Approach and have your fortune told.'

Celeste edged around. An old woman, fitted out in green and purple classic gypsy garb, crooked a gnarled finger, beckoning her near.

'You're lost,' the gypsy predicted above the carnival din, 'but you'll soon find your way.'

Celeste grinned. Of course she looked lost, wandering around, her chin on the ground. Still…

Spotting the crystal ball—much larger and more impressive than the one in the window that day—Celeste drifted over. 'What else do you see?'

The woman's dark eyes gleamed. She dramatically cast age-worn hands over the globe once—twice.

'I see warmth…then cold and hard walls of ice.' Still looking into the glass, her grave expression eased. 'Now I see great warmth return. You think it will burn, but don't be afraid of the new and exciting.' Her eyes slid up to meet Celeste's and she whispered, 'Listen to friendly ghosts.'

Fixed to the spot, Celeste shivered at the same moment the breeze picked up, blowing the hair over her face. When she threw her hair back and turned into the wind rather than against it, Ben was standing there.

He leaned forward.

'*Boo.*'

Celeste jumped out of her skin.

Listen to friendly ghosts?

She spun around. The gypsy straightened her fake wart nose before collecting a rag from under the table to polish her ball. She smiled. 'I do teacup readings too. Otherwise that's two-fifty, hon.'

Feeling like Alice in Wonderland, Celeste rotated back. Gingerly she touched Ben's black crewneck sweater and sighed her relief. He was real.

'Where did you get to?' she croaked, setting a hand against her racing heart.

'I went out to find a café that made a decent coffee. Have you ever tasted hospital instant?' He visibly shuddered. 'I asked the nurse at the station to tell you if I was missed.'

The tension locking Celeste's muscles eased a fraction. He'd left a message but she'd obviously seen a different nurse—the one with the chart.

'When I pulled back into the car park,' he went on, 'you were wandering off down this way. I left the coffees in the car and followed.'

Absorbing each detail, she stroked the sweater he hadn't worn earlier. 'You've changed.'

'I heard on the radio a cold snap's set in. I brought your jacket with me.' He presented it, then walked around to help her into the sleeves. He gave her shoulders a rub and the chill left her bones.

When he stood before her again, they looked into each other's eyes and said together, 'There's something I need to—'

He grinned. 'Ladies first.'

She told the nerves to quit jumping rope in her stomach, then tried to put her feelings into words.

'I've been thinking…about you wanting to return my parents' company…about you racing to bring me here today…about how we might be able to work *us* out.'

Something flared in his eyes, then faded. 'I'll be honest. I don't want my children brought up by anyone but their parents. It's important that a child knows and trusts his mother *and* his father without reserve every day of his life.'

'I agree. As long as it's a joint effort and everyone's happy with the arrangements, including the child.'

He nodded—*good*. 'And, let me say, I have no intention of being a "bring my slippers", "where's my dinner?" type of husband—not next year, not in fifty. You stimulate me—my mind, my body, even my beliefs. I don't want to ever hold you back or hide you away.'

Tears thickened in her throat. He'd touched her more deeply than she'd thought possible. But she had to voice the obvious. 'I bet our parents thought much the same when they agreed to marry.'

'That was their lives and our past.' His expression said he was done with it. 'If we work together—if we *both* want to make this work—we won't regret our decision. I've never loved anyone before. Do you think I'd do anything to lose you?'

Soaking up the raw emotion in his words, she smiled and those tears blurred her vision.

'You love me?'

His chest expanded. 'Completely and for ever. I want to be there for you in everything, whether we have a family or not. You helped open my eyes to so much, most importantly the fact that I can belong. That we belong together.'

Her brow pinched. 'But you do want a family of your own?'

His expression melted. 'Very much. But only with you.'

With curious people milling around, he pulled a jewellery box from his trouser pocket. When the clasp sprang open, the sun hit the rock and threw back a halo of shifting coloured light.

Oh. My.

'I should've thought to present this when I asked you the first time,' he said as he took her hand. 'But now I'm asking again.' His eyes searched hers. 'Celeste, will you marry me?'

She took a breath.

She'd wanted to know what her future held, but

the future was constantly unfolding. All she knew for certain was that she loved this man with everything she was and would ever be. He was right. It was up to them both—two halves of the whole—to move forward together and make certain *they* worked.

She cupped his strong jaw and committed her heart. 'I'd love to marry you. I love you, Ben.' So very much.

Beaming, he slipped the ring on her finger. He gathered her near, but before they sealed her acceptance with a kiss she needed to say—

'I'd like to have a garden ceremony. Is that okay with you?'

He smiled. 'That's fine.' He brought her close again.

'And I think we should make a pact not to work on weekends. All work and no play…'

'A couple needs time together.' He nodded. 'Done.'

Hugging her extra tight, he slanted his mouth over hers. Her hand shot up, blocking his lips from capturing hers.

'Ben, there's one more thing…'

He caught her hand and smiled a sexy smile that made everything but him, and his obvious love for her, fade away. 'Honey, now would be a good time to let me kiss you so we can get on with our happily ever after.'

She smiled. He was right.

So she did.

EPILOGUE

Three years later.

SITTING at her home-office desk, Celeste clicked open the appropriate spreadsheet and typed the long-time client's name in the 'special order' header.

She collected the handpiece and set it to her ear again. 'So, you'd like lilies and freesias on the tables. No, I think that will work beautifully for a birthday celebration. Special bouquets for the mums? I love it. I have their favourites on file—'

A soft cry caught her ear and Celeste stilled.

'Nicole, sorry, can I call you back?' She laughed. 'Yes, it's the baby. I knew you'd understand. I'll email a price first thing in the morning.'

After disconnecting, Celeste rolled back her chair and headed for the adjoining room.

Star Arrangements was going ahead in leaps and bounds. Awards, international orders, A-list clients, as well as a number of charities she regularly helped with special events and sponsorships. All her goals regarding business had been achieved. But she'd fulfilled another, even more amazing dream.

She eased back the gliding doors and hurried through the semi darkness to her gorgeous one-year-old daughter. Standing in her cot, holding a rung with one tiny hand, rubbing a sleepy eye with the other, Ava Krystal yawned and grumbled. But when she saw her visitor, her face lit up.

'Mum-mum.'

Heart so full it sometimes ached, Celeste collected her baby at the same time the second set of adjoining doors slid open.

Ben strode in, surveyed the shadowed room, then smiled seeing mother with child.

He joined them and tickled Ava's chin. 'Hey, sweetie. You're supposed to be asleep.' He kissed his wife on the lips, his mouth lingering before he drew reluctantly away. 'You finish what you're doing. I can put her back to sleep.'

Still tingling from his kiss, Celeste caught the time on the unicorn clock on the dresser. Ten past eight. That late!

Ava stretched, reaching one hand out towards Daddy while holding onto her mummy's hair with the other. Celeste kissed her baby's chubby cheek. 'It's fine. I'm well and truly done for the day.'

She was glad tomorrow was Friday; she would work an hour in the morning, then it was family time right through until Tuesday. With Ben's chock-a-block investment portfolio, he mostly worked from home as well, organising his hours largely around family needs. Saturday they planned to go to the zoo—a first for little Ava. A first for Ben, too.

She finger-combed Ava's blonde curls. Knowing the game, with some indecipherable word, Ava tried to catch her mother's hand. Laughing, Celeste softly bopped her baby's nose.

Wanting to join in, Ben had put out his arms at the same time his cell phone rang. He checked the screen, then thumbed a button and clipped the phone back on his belt.

'You can see to that.' Celeste cuddled Ava, who cuddled back. 'I'll read Munchkin her favourite book.'

Ben's broad-shouldered silhouette crossed to the bookshelf. 'New York can wait. We'll both read to Ava.'

Liking the idea, Celeste moved to the comfy twin couch in the corner. Ben joined them and ten minutes after reading about fairies and magic mice, Ava was sleeping again.

Gazing down at his daughter, Ben looped an arm around Celeste's shoulder and absently twirled a wave with his finger. 'I can't wait till she's old enough to throw a ball,' he whispered.

She let her head rock back and his fingers strummed more of her hair, then settled on her shoulder. So nice.

'I'll leave that to you,' she whispered back. 'I've got my hand up for painting lessons.'

'I'm a whiz at stick figures, if that's any help.'

She looked over. 'It's not.'

His eyes turned hot and he grinned. 'You know what else I'm a whiz at?'

She shrugged, playing dumb. He moved close to nuzzle her ear and delicious longing kicked off through her veins, sweeping like a storm through her body.

She closed her eyes and sighed. 'Oh, yes, I remember now.'

His lips trailed her neck. 'Let's put the baby to bed.'

Carefully they moved together to the cot. Celeste lay Ava down, Ben tucked her in. So strong yet caring beside her, he looped an arm around her waist and drew her near.

'I love being a dad.'

Smiling, Celeste leant into him, forever thankful they'd believed in their love and had become engaged then married. They worked everything out together and it worked very well. Gerard, Rhyll and Ben's siblings were regular visitors to their home, just as Rodney, Suzanne and dear little Tiegan were. In fact, Tiegan stayed over at least one night a month. She'd asked to stay the whole weekend next time, and everyone, including Ava, had cheered.

Past the cot, the curtains were drawn apart. Beyond the wall-to-wall window, the night sky twinkled unbelievably bright.

'Any falling stars?' he asked.

For some reason Celeste thought of PLM, which she'd sold not long before they'd been married. The proceeds were in a bank account, ready for Ava when she reached twenty-one. Anita would have approved.

She sighed and burrowed into her husband's strong arm and chest. 'I don't need falling stars. There's nothing more I could wish for.'

He turned her into his embrace and, angling her chin, kissed her with all the emotion she also felt burning inside—passion, deepest longing, made stronger by trust and respect.

When his mouth gradually left hers, he searched her eyes. 'I love you.'

She smiled. 'I love you, too.'

It was that simple. And tonight, tomorrow—for the rest of their lives—nothing would matter more.

* * * * *

Harlequin is 60 years old,
and Harlequin Blaze is celebrating!
After all, a lot can happen in 60 years,
or 60 minutes…or 60 seconds!
Find out what's going down in Blaze's
heart-stopping new mini-series,
FROM 0 TO 60!
Getting from "Hello" to "How was it?"
can happen fast….

Here's a sneak peek of the first book,
A LONG HARD RIDE
by Alison Kent
Available March 2009

"Is that for me?" Trey asked.

Cardin Worth cocked her head to the side and considered how much better the day already seemed. "Good morning to you, too."

When she didn't hold out the second cup of coffee for him to take, he came closer. She sipped from her heavy white mug, hiding her grin and her giddy rush of nerves behind it.

But when he stopped in front of her, she made the mistake of lowering her gaze from his face to the exposed strip of his chest. It was either give him his cup of coffee or bury her nose against him and breathe in. She remembered so clearly how he smelled. How he tasted.

She gave him his coffee.

After taking a quick gulp, he smiled and said, "Good morning, Cardin. I hope the floor wasn't too hard for you."

The hardness of the floor hadn't been the

problem. She shook her head. "Are you kidding? I slept like a baby, swaddled in my sleeping bag."

"In my sleeping bag, you mean."

If he wanted to get technical, yeah. "Thanks for the loaner. It made sleeping on the floor almost bearable." As had the warmth of his spooned body, she thought, then quickly changed the subject. "I saw you have a loaf of bread and some eggs. Would you like me to cook breakfast?"

He lowered his coffee mug slowly, his gaze as warm as the sun on her shoulders, as the ceramic heating her hands. "I didn't bring you out here to wait on me."

"You didn't bring me out here at all. I volunteered to come."

"To help me get ready for the race. Not to serve me."

"It's just breakfast, Trey. And coffee." Even if last night it had been more. Even if the way he was looking at her made her want to climb back into that sleeping bag. "I work much better when my stomach's not growling. I thought it might be the same for you."

"It is, but I'll cook. You made the coffee."

"That's because I can't work at all without caffeine."

"If I'd known that, I would've put on a pot as soon I got up."

"What time *did* you get up?" Judging by the sun's position, she swore it couldn't be any later than seven now. And, yeah, they'd agreed to start working at six.

"Maybe four?" he guessed, giving her a lazy smile.

"But it was almost two…" She let the sentence

dangle, finishing the thought privately. She was quite sure he knew exactly what time they'd finally fallen asleep after he'd made love to her.

The question facing her now was where did this relationship—if you could even call it *that*—go from here?

* * * * *

Cardin and Trey are about to find out that great
sex is only the beginning....
Don't miss the fireworks!
Get ready for
A LONG HARD RIDE
by Alison Kent
Available March 2009,
wherever Blaze books are sold.

HARLEQUIN *Presents*

*Introducing an exciting debut
from Harlequin Presents!*

Indulge yourself with this intense story
of passion, blackmail and seduction.

VALENTI'S
ONE-MONTH MISTRESS
by Sabrina Philips

Faye fell for the sensual Dante Valenti—but he
took her virginity and left her heartbroken. She
swore *never again!* But he wants her back,
and what Dante wants, Dante takes....

Book #2808

Available March 2009

Look out for more titles from Sabrina Philips
coming soon to Harlequin Presents!

REQUEST YOUR FREE BOOKS!

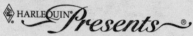 HARLEQUIN *Presents*

PASSION
GUARANTEED
SEDUCTION

2 FREE NOVELS
PLUS 2
FREE GIFTS!

YES! Please send me 2 FREE Harlequin Presents® novels and my 2 FREE gifts (gifts are worth about $10). After receiving them, if I don't wish to receive any more books, I can return the shipping statement marked "cancel". If I don't cancel, I will receive 6 brand-new novels every month and be billed just $4.05 per book in the U.S. or $4.74 per book in Canada, plus 25¢ shipping and handling per book and applicable taxes, if any*. That's a savings of close to 15% off the cover price! I understand that accepting the 2 free books and gifts places me under no obligation to buy anything. I can always return a shipment and cancel at any time. Even if I never buy another book, the two free books and gifts are mine to keep forever.

106 HDN ERRW   306 HDN ERRL

Name _____ (PLEASE PRINT)

Address _____ Apt. #

City _____ State/Prov. _____ Zip/Postal Code

Signature (if under 18, a parent or guardian must sign)

Mail to the **Harlequin Reader Service:**
IN U.S.A.: P.O. Box 1867, Buffalo, NY 14240-1867
IN CANADA: P.O. Box 609, Fort Erie, Ontario L2A 5X3
Not valid to current subscribers of Harlequin Presents books.

Want to try two free books from another line?
Call 1-800-873-8635 or visit www.morefreebooks.com.

* Terms and prices subject to change without notice. N.Y. residents add applicable sales tax. Canadian residents will be charged applicable provincial taxes and GST. Offer not valid in Quebec. This offer is limited to one order per household. All orders subject to approval. Credit or debit balances in a customer's account(s) may be offset by any other outstanding balance owed by or to the customer. Please allow 4 to 6 weeks for delivery. Offer available while quantities last.

Your Privacy: Harlequin Books is committed to protecting your privacy. Our Privacy Policy is available online at www.eHarlequin.com or upon request from the Reader Service. From time to time we make our lists of customers available to reputable third parties who may have a product or service of interest to you. If you would prefer we not share your name and address, please check here. ☐

HP08R

I ♥ HARLEQUIN® *Presents*

BROUGHT TO YOU BY FANS OF
HARLEQUIN PRESENTS.

We are its editors and authors
and biggest fans—and we'd
love to hear from YOU!

Subscribe today to our online blog at
www.iheartpresents.com